20 Greatest Revolutionaries

Kalyani Mookherji is an alumnus of Jadavpur University, Kolkata, from where she finished her postgraduation in English Literature. She has been a writer and educator for over ten years now.

This book attests to her keen interest in what goes into the making of famous revolutionaries as well as the evolution of revolutionary ideals like equality and liberty.

Despite being a busy mom to a bright teen and a spoilt dog, she finds time for other interests like music, baking and blogging at crumbsonmynotebook.wordpress.com

20 Greatest REVOLUTIONARIES

KALYANI MOOKHERJI

RUPA

Published by
Rupa Publications India Pvt. Ltd 2019
7/16, Ansari Road, Daryaganj
New Delhi 110002

Sales centres:
Allahabad Bengaluru Chennai
Hyderabad Jaipur Kathmandu
Kolkata Mumbai

Copyright © Kalyani Mookherji 2019

The views and opinions expressed in this book are the author's own and the facts are as reported by her which have been verified to the extent possible, and the publishers are not in any way liable for the same.

All rights reserved.

No part of this publication may be reproduced, transmitted, or stored in a retrieval system, in any form or by any means, electronic, mechanical, photocopying, recording or otherwise, without the prior permission of the publisher.

ISBN: 978-93-5333-526-7

First impression 2019

10 9 8 7 6 5 4 3 2 1

The moral right of the author has been asserted.

Printed by HT Media Ltd, Gr. Noida

This book is sold subject to the condition that it shall not, by way of trade or otherwise, be lent, resold, hired out, or otherwise circulated, without the publisher's prior consent, in any form of binding or cover other than that in which it is published.

For Ma and Baba,
who lived through many revolutions
of their own — big and small.

Contents

Introduction	ix
1. George Washington	1
2. Toussaint L'Ouverture	9
3. Maximilien Robespierre	17
4. Simón Bolívar	27
5. Rani Lakshmibai	38
6. Emmeline Pankhurst	46
7. Mahatma Gandhi	53
8. Vladimir Lenin	64
9. Mao Zedong	75
10. Ho Chi Minh	88
11. Subhas Chandra Bose	99
12. Michael Collins	109
13. Birsa Munda	117
14. Mustafa Kemal Atatürk	123

15. Josip Broz Tito	132
16. Nelson Mandela	139
17. Che Guevara	145
18. Fidel Castro	154
19. Aung San Suu Kyi	162
20. Ayatollah Khomeini	170
Conclusion	175
Acknowledgements	179

Introduction

'It was the best of times, it was the worst of times, it was the age of wisdom, it was the age of foolishness, it was the epoch of belief, it was the epoch of incredulity...'

The literary classic, *A Tale of Two Cities*, opens with these timeless lines, giving a trenchant description of the French Revolution, and indeed, all revolutions in general. In fact, Dickens' words ring true of even the Industrial Revolution that took place around a century later, and from which the modern era is roughly dated.

In keeping with its meaning, the Industrial Revolution transformed practically every aspect of society—how people lived, worked, interacted, enjoyed themselves and ruled others. Among its most significant consequences was the dominance of the capitalist system in the economy. This, together with the corresponding political structures like colonialism and imperialism, created new inequalities and widened some old ones in different parts of the world.

On the other side of this simmering cauldron of regional

or national discontent was a new consciousness of liberal or egalitarian philosophies. Like the Industrial Revolution, these mostly emerged from Western Europe, either in the writings of Locke, Paine and Mill or in those of Marx and Engels. Naturally, not everyone in oppressed communities had equal access to these inspiring words, nor were they made of equal mettle which would make them use such resources without fear and weakness. Also, a revolutionary had to be a people person—imbued with inborn charisma that would move masses, and irradiated with personal dynamism that would inspire courage and commitment to a difficult cause. Thus, a modern revolutionary could be born only when the right personality met the right resources to rise against conditions of inequality and oppression.

But what makes for a revolution in the first place? Upon examining various definitions, a revolution can be understood to be a mass uprising over issues that affect the majority of society, usually marked by armed struggle, resulting in an overhauling of prevailing political as well as related establishments.

With this interpretation as the benchmark, the present book mines modern history for the 20 greatest revolutionaries. Since it holds popular appeal and mass involvement as crucial to the definition of a revolution, drivers of coup d'états and palace intrigues are not included as revolutionary figures.

INTRODUCTION

According to some experts, a revolution is a phenomenon that simmers and then quickly comes to a climactic stage. If so, it would rule out long-drawn movements led by the likes of Mahatma Gandhi and Aung San Suu Kyi. However, the impact of their struggle has been so wide-ranging and decisive with regard to the history of their people that it qualifies such movements for the most important trait of a revolution—leading to transformation of the existing political system. Indeed, though largely non-violent, these revolutions still involved some degree of armed conflict. Gandhi, for example, called upon Indians to 'do or die' at the launch of the Quit India Movement in 1942, just as Suu Kyi's National League for Democracy (NLD) supporters retaliated with arms against the brutal repression of the Burmese military junta in 2003.

The greatest difficulty in determining the twenty names in this book was to reconcile the popularity of figures like Rani Lakshmibai in the public domain with the absence of their immediate impact on society in terms of new laws, new political systems and so on—something that the comparatively lesser known Birsa Munda had. But even though Rani Lakshmibai's battle against the British soldiers did not lead to transformation of any social or political institution right away, the physical and moral bravery displayed by her and others during the Rebellion of 1857 has rightly led the struggle to be described as India's first war of independence.

And finally, because the book talks about the greatest revolutionaries, those figures who were later discredited by their own people like Mugabe and Gaddafi have been left out.

So much for the rationale behind the book's inclusion of these 20 figures among the greatest revolutionaries of the world. At the end of the long, blood-soaked day, it is not so much the gender, the age or the class that matters in the making of a revolutionary but who lies down to wear and who rises up to break the fetters that bind one to the ground.

1. George Washington

The acrid smell of burning flesh went unnoticed; the roar of cannons went unheard — the man at the centre of it all had his gaze fixed on the horizon. This was George Washington, Commander-in-Chief of the colonial forces at the Battle of Yorktown which he would win before the sun set that day on 19 October 1781. Washington was the most important figure in the American Revolutionary War that led to America successfully breaking away from British colonial control. He would go on to become the first president of the United States (US), for two terms, and eventually be hailed as the Father of the Nation.

Early Life

Born on 22 February 1732 at Westmoreland County in the American state of Virginia, Washington spent the early days of his childhood on the family-owned Ferry Farm opposite Fredericksburg, Virginia. His father was an enterprising man who, after some years at sea, had settled down to a planter's life on the American East Coast. Unfortunately, he died when Washington was just eleven, after which the young boy was brought up by his older half-brother, Lawrence.

In Lawrence's family, young Washington was exposed to a bigger world and finer ways. He received formal schooling till fifteen, after which he became a land surveyor — a profession that would come in handy years later while he studied battlefield conditions to determine the course of wars. Additionally, it taught him physical and psychological resilience that would again see him through many tough conditions in the future.

Success as a Planter

After Lawrence died in 1752 of tuberculosis and his only daughter Sarah too died within two months, Washington came to inherit his stepbrother's fertile plantation, including the manor known as Mount Vernon. For the next two decades, Washington worked assiduously as a farmer, expanding the estates, improving the house as well as bringing in many farming innovations. Backed by his success on land and in several sports like riding, hunting and fishing, Washington soon became popular in the local community as a sociable and enterprising planter.

However, Washington craved for more—action as well as new experience. The opportunity came, when, in the mid-eighteenth century, the French colonials began encroaching in the Ohio Valley lands, previously claimed by the British Crown. The ensuing hostilities between the British and the French colonial forces came to be known as the French and Indian War, since the French were supported by some American-Indian tribes. Though Washington, fighting on the side of the Crown, did not achieve spectacular military success, he proved his endurance and determination to see a project through. Also, the military expeditions laid bare the injustice of the superior command of British officers over colonial officers—a discrimination that would feed into Washington's revolutionary fire.

After settling back at Mount Vernon, Washington got married to a wealthy widow named Martha Dandridge who brought with her large estates owned by her deceased husband, Daniel Parke Custis. Washington was now kept doubly busy—supervising his own, as well as the Custis estates, at the White House on the York River. As a result, in the 1750s and '60s, Washington became the largest and richest planter in the whole of Virginia. In order to fulfil his political ambitions, he also served in the House of Burgesses, a colonial legislature in Virginia.

In 1764, the British government began imposing heavy taxes on its American colonies as a way of raising revenues.

An example of popular opposition to these harsh taxes was the Boston Tea Party in which American patriots disguised as Mohawk Indians dumped 342 chests of tea belonging to the British East India Company into the Boston Harbour on 16 December 1773. The rally of 'no taxation without representation' grew louder, and in 1774, the Virginia provincial convention elected Washington as one of the seven delegates to the First Continental Congress.

Leadership of the Revolutionary War

Anticipating the inevitability of an armed conflict between the forces of the American colonials and the Crown, Washington returned to Virginia and began training troops. He set out for Philadelphia again to attend the Second Continental Congress of March 1775, which eventually decided to grant him the supreme military command of all colonial forces, known as the Continental Army.

It was no easy task. The maximum strength of the colonial army was a little more than 20,000. Washington set about to discipline the army and train it with modern weapons even as he solved disputes among subordinates. Despite early difficulties, Washington managed to keep his forces together through five years of revolutionary war against the forces of the Crown. Eventually, he proved his strategic skills with surprise attacks of the Crown-held garrisons at Trenton on 26 December 1776 and then less than a month later, again, at Princeton on 3 January 1777. These successes restored the flagging morale of the Continental forces.

However, continuous bad weather, poor supplies and semi-starvation through the winter of 1777–78, as well as a lack of support from the Congress put the greatest strain on Washington's leadership and endurance. Finally, with the French switching sides from the Crown to the Americans in early 1781, Washington regained his footing in the war. His strategic vision and committed leadership in the Battle of Yorktown succeeded in compelling Lord Cornwallis, the commander of the British forces, to surrender on 19 October 1781. After quelling a near-mutiny by discontented soldiers whose pay had been delayed, Washington resigned his commission to the Continental Congress at the state senate chamber of Maryland, Annapolis, amidst the expression of gratitude of an entire nation.

Presidential Tenures

For the next four years, Washington got busy supervising his estates from his home at Mount Vernon. He kept an open house since close friends, officials, old comrades from the army as well as visitors from other states and countries often dropped by.

As a measure of the high social and political standing

that Washington enjoyed in his community, he was elected to the Constitutional Convention in 1787, and served as its presiding officer too. His support to the new Constitution was crucial to its acceptance by all members of the Convention, and eventually by all states. When the matter of the first president of the newly-formed United States of America came up, Washington was once again the natural choice. He alone commanded the support of all political dispensations at home, and the utmost respect abroad. No sooner was his first presidential term—from 1789 to 1793—over than he was again elected for a second presidential term from 1794 to 1797. During his presidential tenures Washington tried to remain equidistant from the Republicans and the Federalists, although historians note that he leaned a little towards the latter. Washington supported the founding of the Bank of the United States as well as Hamilton's proposal for the federal assumption of state debts, and overall was in favour of a strong federal government. At the same time, he pursued a policy of strict neutrality in foreign affairs, and, in fact, even refused to take sides upon the outbreak of hostilities between France and England in 1793.

Equally importantly, for a nation that had just eschewed all royal connections, Washington saw the need for America to establish its own identity and protocol. Thus, as the first couple, he and his wife took to travelling in a coach drawn by four or six smart horses, replete with richly-liveried outriders and lackeys. Additionally, for all formal events, he would be dressed in a black velvet suit with gold buckles and would entertain solemnly but uniformly.

Death and Legacy

Though pressed with a third term, Washington graciously refused, and retired to his old home in Mount Vernon. On 14 December 1799, after struggling with an acute throat infection, George Washington passed away. Upon his death, all slaves owned by him were legally freed, just like his wife freed slaves of the Custis estate.

Among all the Founding Fathers, George Washington towered over everyone else. His leadership was not just crucial in winning military battles, but more importantly, in holding disparate forces together—both on the battlefield as well as during his two presidential tenures. Thus, the man who sired no biological children came to be revered as the Father of the Nation.

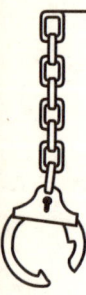

Fascinating Facts

- Stories about Washington's childhood—like that of him chopping down the cherry tree and then coming clean about it—were popularized by writers like Mason Locke Weems. Such stories were largely fictitious, nevertheless, they helped make up for the lack of biographical information on the leader's early childhood.
- As a president, Washington cultivated several mannerisms of the royalty—he stopped shaking hands and acknowledged greetings with a slight bow. Also, on state occasions, he would meet guests while standing on a raised platform.
- Through his adult life, Washington suffered from toothaches; by fifty-seven, he had got all his teeth out and wore artificial dentures of ivory set in silver plate.

2. Toussaint L'Ouverture

Within the chilly walls of Fort de Joux, a short and homely-looking man was lost in thought. The rough draft of a memoir lay open before him, but his mind was racing back to the days on plantations where he had made the incredible journey from a slave to a free man, and then to the leader of all of Hispaniola, the second-largest island of the West Indies. The man was Toussaint L'Ouverture, under whose leadership Haiti became the first place in the New World to officially end slavery. Though he would not live to see it, Haiti would go on to become the first free black state in 1804.

Early Life

Born as François Dominique Toussaint in 1743 at Breda, near Cap-Français, Saint-Domingue, the future leader grew up in a slave family on one of the many sugar plantations that existed on the French colony. What worked in his favour was an upbringing by an educated father and then learning some French from the Jesuits. Coupled with his own initiative, L'Ouverture quickly won the patronage of the manager of the plantation and became its livestock handler, then coachman, and eventually earned the influential position of steward.

In 1776, L'Ouverture legally obtained his freedom. He got married and had two sons, thus settling down into domestic life. However, in August 1791, a slave revolt broke out in the northern part of the island and soon spread to several places. Even as the rebellion gathered into its fold thousands of slaves desperate to overthrow a life of exploitation, L'Ouverture initially remained unaffected.

News about his former master caught up in the violence finally forced L'Ouverture to act. Revolting slaves were indiscriminately killing any European or mulatto — people of mixed racial ancestry — who happened to come their way. Wading into this mayhem, L'Ouverture helped his former master escape, but at the same time, realized the need to put an end to the heinous system of slavery on the island.

L'Ouverture took charge. He was aware that he could do a much better job of leading the people, as compared to the current leaders of the rebellion. He raised his own army and trained it in guerrilla tactics. It was around this time that he adopted the title of L'Ouverture—meaning 'opening' in French—perhaps as a way of indicating that he was the person to open possibilities of freedom and self-governance to the people of the island.

Rise to Military Power

With France getting caught up in a military conflict with Spain, the black commanders of the slave rebellion saw the practicality of aligning themselves with the enemy's enemy—in this case, Spain, which was in control of the eastern two-thirds of Hispaniola, then called Santo Domingo, and now known as the Dominican Republic. L'Ouverture was consequently knighted, and made a general by the Spaniards. He carried out a successful military campaign in the north of the island which, along with mulatto victories in the south as well as the British landing on the coasts, spelled disaster for French rulers.

The astute leader that L'Ouverture was, he realized that seeking victory over the entire island with the help of Spain or Britain would be akin to changing one master for another. Also, unlike the British and the Spaniards, the French National Convention had abolished slavery. Thus, true to his title, he made the bold step of opening negotiations with the French in May 1794, and convinced the governor, Étienne Laveaux, to make him the lieutenant governor and the de facto ruler of Saint-Domingue.

L'Ouverture knew that it was not enough to acquire power—he would have to ensure that potential enemies were eliminated, so that his rule could be stable. The British and the Spaniards, whose help he had earlier sought, were roundly defeated, at times with brutal force. Next, L'Ouverture set about strengthening the economy of the island. Émigrés (Frenchmen who fled France after the French Revolution) who had been expelled from France were invited to Saint-Domingue to take over the plantations. Though L'Ouverture freed the slaves, he also realized the need to retain Europeans and mulattoes for their economic capital. The slaves were allowed a share in the plantation profits, but sometimes they were also compelled to work on the lines of military discipline. Legally, the slaves were now equal to other social classes, and yet, L'Ouverture believed that the African-origin population could learn from its former European masters.

This careful balancing act underlined L'Ouverture's domestic and foreign policies. Actually, it was borne out of a need for practicality—he was determined not to allow a return of slavery, but realized the necessity for economic alliances with the very colonial powers that allowed slavery in their colonies. Thus, he signed commercial treaties with Britain and America which allowed the export of sugar in return for weapons and other goods.

With France, L'Ouverture maintained an outward allegiance, though he disposed a series of governors from whom he sensed even the slightest hint of trouble. In the process, he even took over the southern part of the island which had been governed by the semi-independent mulatto leader, Andre Rigaud.

Complete Control of Hispaniola

The eastern part of Hispaniola had been under the rule of Spain which still followed slavery as an official policy. L'Ouverture was not only determined to eliminate slavery from the entire island but saw this as an opportunity to do away with all possible sources of opposition to his power. Thus, defying Napoleon Bonaparte himself, L'Ouverture invaded Santo Domingo in January 1801 and freed the slaves. He was now in complete control of Hispaniola and ordered it to be ruled under a new constitution, according to which he would be the governor general for life. In evidence of his acute statesmanship, he ensured that no harm would come to European planters and mulattoes; he decreed Catholicism to be the official religion of Hispaniola in conscious rejection of voodoo practices. Even though he made many public overtures of allegiance to Bonaparte, he declared himself a Frenchman so that there would be no need for the constitutional provision of Hispaniola being ruled by a representative from France.

L'Ouverture's policies of compromise bought him some time. Though Bonaparte ostensibly approved of the Haitian leader's ascension, he secretly disliked the blacks, and planned to re-establish Saint-Domingue as a French colony. L'Ouverture, too, was rightly suspicious of Bonaparte's intentions, and began amassing a huge trained army to fight the French. The people of the island were likewise divided—while the Europeans and mulattoes wanted a return of French rule, other black leaders wanted to take over all plantations and divide them amongst themselves. Eventually, their mutual suspicion grew stronger and headed towards the inevitable confrontation.

Final Conflict

In January 1802, General Charles Leclerc launched a French invasion, actively supported by European and mulatto settlers, that even garnered the support of black leaders like Christophe and Dessalines. Outnumbered by his opponents, L'Ouverture decided to surrender in May, on the condition that the French General would not bring back slavery on the island. Initially the Haitian leader was allowed to retire to a plantation, but in the following month, he was tricked into captivity and exiled to Fort-de-Joux in the French Jura Mountains. There L'Ouverture remained, far away from his beloved Saint-Domingue, till he finally succumbed to relentless interrogation in April 1803.

Legacy

Later historians have latched on to L'Ouverture's policy of practicality and accused him of double standards — even as he freed the slaves across Saint-Domingue, he ensured the quick dismissal of any potential opponents. Also, while he used British and Spanish help initially to pressurize the French, he lost no time in turning against the same allies to ensure a smooth compromise with French representatives. The fact was that such duality was necessary to be able to maintain a precarious balance between freedom and economic survival.

Though, eventually, L'Ouverture was betrayed by his own commanders as much as by the French, the Haitian Revolution that he led actually set in motion a series of events that had a wide-ranging impact on the New World. Because of the Haitian conflict, Napoleon agreed to let go of Louisiana in North America. More significantly, L'Ouverture came to be enshrined as the iconic liberator of slaves, not only in literature and culture — as evident in Wordsworth's poem, 'To Toussaint L'Ouverture' — but also in actual history as an inspiration for American abolitionists and Latin American freedom fighters over the next century. Above all, because of L'Ouverture's leadership and vision, Hispaniola emerged as the first black island to gain independence from European colonizers.

20 GREATEST REVOLUTIONARIES

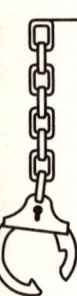

Fascinating Facts

▶ During his slave days, L'Ouverture's knowledge of medicinal plants helped him to work as a healer on the plantation.

▶ L'Ouverture was also known for his horsemanship, a skill that suited his short, stocky build and was useful during his military campaigns.

3. Maximilien Robespierre

His jaw throbbed with a dull pain but it was nothing compared to the distress he felt at the sight ahead. He could not understand how the very populace for whom he had fought all his life now cheered at his execution. The guillotine blade glinted in the sun; he told himself, 'All will be over soon,' and thus ended the life of one of the foremost revolutionaries of the French Revolution. Though historians have pointed out his role in the Reign of Terror, he is also remembered for leading the transformation of France from a monarchy to a republic, as well as introducing widespread socio-economic reforms.

Early Life

Born as Maximilien François Marie Isidore de Robespierre on 6 May 1758 into a doctor's family in the French town of Arras, the future revolutionary grew up to be a brilliant student. While studying at the Collège d'Arras, run by the Oratorians, he won a scholarship to the reputed Parisian college of Louis-le-Grand. There he studied law and philosophy, earning his degree in the former in 1781. Upon completing his education, Robespierre returned to Arras and set up a profitable private practice. Soon he was successful enough to get an appointment as a judge at the Salle Épiscopale. This court gave him jurisdiction over the provostship of the diocese. He took a keen interest in the affairs of the people of the district.

Growing Activism

Robespierre's growing professional reputation earned him a place in the Arras Academy where he went on to become the chancellor, and eventually its president as well. However, he continued to reach out to the ordinary people and often provided free legal services to the needy. During this time he wrote powerful pamphlets — like the 'Report on Degrading Punishments' — denouncing the exploitation of the poor under laws made by the wealthy ruling classes. An even more disruptive piece of writing was the 'Report for Lord Dupond' in which Robespierre criticized the arbitrary nature of judgements as well as unfair aristocratic privileges.

With the summoning of the Estate General in 1789 for

a meeting, Robespierre wrote yet another pamphlet titled 'To the People of Artois on the Necessity of Reforming the Estates of Artois', which highlighted the need for social and economic change in favour of the commoners or the third estate. Not surprisingly, he was chosen by the people of Arras as one of their representatives, as well as one of the eight deputies from Artois.

Political Ascendency

With the convening of the National Assembly, Robespierre came to be famous for his powerful speeches, driving home the need to abolish royal privileges and give the common people their due. Given his extremist views, Robespierre aroused intense opposition, especially from the royalist segment of the Assembly. As a result, he was not allowed to be part of most legislative committees. Though he was expressly barred from the presidency of the National Assembly, such was his growing popularity that, in June 1790, the National Assembly was compelled to elect him as its secretary. Shortly afterwards, he was also appointed a judge of the Versailles tribunal.

Around the same time, Paris was witnessing the rise of a radical political group that called itself the Jacobins. Members of this party strongly advocated a return to the original ideals of the French Revolution encompassed in the slogan, 'Liberté, égalité, fraternité', which meant liberty for all people, complete equality of all classes and brotherhood among all. This brought the Jacobins in direct opposition to the supporters of royal privilege. Though initially the club was only open to the deputies, with increasing popularity it began admitting non-deputies as well. In April 1790, Robespierre was elected its president, and by July the same year, its membership had swelled to 1200, including intellectuals and even successful bourgeoisie citizens.

Support to the New Constitution

In order to prevent the gains made by the French Revolution from being frittered away, Robespierre hastened the approval of the new constitution. This was based on the ideals of the French philosophers of the Age of Enlightenment like Rousseau, Montesquieu and Voltaire. Of particular note was the Declaration of the Rights of Man and of the Citizen that formed the preamble to the constitution. More importantly, Robespierre insisted that all laws of the land should ensure that the rights safeguarded in the Declaration were not compromised. This was a major change in the sociopolitical dispensation of the French governance.

Robespierre, around this time, also pushed for a whole range of reforms like universal suffrage, which would extend voting to all social classes. He also advocated the ending of racial and religious discrimination, which meant freeing of African slaves and the return of certain civic rights to the Jews. More significantly, he opposed many of the prevailing barriers to socio-economic advancement, saying that employment to public offices, the National Guard as well the commissioned ranks in the army, should be thrown open to all. He defended the common people's right to petition as well as the reunion of the province, Avignon, with France in September 1791. Like a true Jacobin, Robespierre was vehemently opposed to all forms of aristocratic privilege, like the royal veto, as well as the arbitrary power of ministers.

Around this time, Paris was fast spiralling into chaos. The French monarch Louis XVI fled the capital in June 1791, and the ensuing uncertainty split the National Assembly into two broad halves—one was made up of Moderates like Lafayette who were open to the continuation of monarchy, while the other was composed of Jacobins who wanted a complete change to a republican France. For some time, Robespierre even had to go into hiding to save his life, but with the dissolution of the National Assembly, he returned to a triumphant reception in Paris.

Abolition of Monarchy

The landscape of anarchy was soon darkened by threats of invasion from Austria and Prussia. On 5 September

1792, in the backdrop of all these troubles, Robespierre was elected by the people of Paris to head the delegation to the National Convention. This was a group of elected representatives from France tasked with the governance of the country. However, the National Convention was divided into two opposing groups. One was made up of the moderate Girondins who supported the monarchy and dominated the government as well as the bureaucracy. The other, led by Robespierre, comprised of the Jacobins who were in favour of abolishing monarchy.

Moved by Robespierre's influential journal titled *Letters to His Constituents*, as well as a stirring speech given on 3 December 1792, the National Convention finally agreed to abolish monarchy. King Louis XVI was brought to trial for acts of treason against the state, and finally executed in January 1794.

Spread of Anarchy

If anything, the king's execution only worsened the conflict between the Girondins and the Jacobins, which was symbolic of the entire society sinking into anarchy. In the ensuing power struggle, Robespierre rallied his Parisian supporters and led the overthrow of Girondins as well as the arrest of their prominent leaders.

In April 1794, as a desperate attempt to stem the growing chaos, a Committee of Public Safety was formed, and in June, Robespierre himself took charge. In the face of riots breaking out due to food shortage, he was desperate to enforce order. Equally worrying was the coalition of foreign powers readying to attack the French borders. Faced with threats from within and without, the committee ordered the arrest and execution of anyone even remotely suspected of opposing the revolution. This led to large-scale violence and senseless massacres that collectively came to be dubbed as the Reign of Terror.

New Religion

Robespierre realized that continuous negation of life — as symbolized by the Reign of Terror — would sooner or later lead to annihilation of all that was still good and virtuous. He thus appealed to the essential life principle in human nature and called for the establishment of a new religion. Unlike the ultra-rationalists and the anti-Christianity movement that made up the highly radical fringe groups, Robespierre affirmed the existence of God. At the same time, realizing the need to depart from the mainstream Church that had long supported the exploitative feudal system in France, he propounded a new civic religion based on the cult of the Supreme Being.

The Beginning of the End

From mid-1794, it became clear that Robespierre's power was on the decline. The erstwhile Girondins and other moderates like Georges Danton already blamed him for the large-scale violence of the Reign of Terror. Now ultra-radical leaders like Jacques Herbert accused him of not being democratic enough. Added to this was Robespierre's own failing health brought on by long years of living in strain and surrounded by violence. Worst of all was his steady loss of popularity in Paris where people continued to struggle with food shortages and general economic difficulties. The unleashing of yet another wave of violence in the summer of 1794, dubbed the Great Terror, further broke Robespierre's will, and here on he remained a largely passive spectator to the insurgents' growing power.

By the time insurgents held him hostage in the Hotel de Ville in 27 July 1794, Robespierre did not even have the will to rally for reinforcements from the Paris Commune. Injured by a bullet to his jaw, Robespierre was arrested by the soldiers of the National Convention. Finally, on 28 July, he, along with twenty-one of his closest associates, was guillotined before a cheering mob on the Place de la Revolution.

Legacy

Much has been written about the excesses of the Reign of Terror and Robespierre's role in it. However, some historians have also pointed out that Robespierre himself was sickened by the large-scale massacres and did his best to drill some sense into his officials, and even demanded their dismissal for 'dishonouring the Revolution'. Robespierre himself passed orders to protect those deputies who had opposed the arrest of the Girondins and had tried to save the king's sister.

Far more enduring has been Robespierre's legacy in realizing the essential ideals of the French Revolution. He strived to bring about a more egalitarian society and open up socio-economic opportunities long denied to common people. Till the end, he believed in the vision of a republican France, which eventually came through, as we see in history.

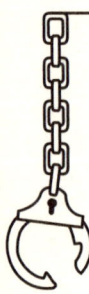

Fascinating Facts

- To celebrate his new religion, Robespierre organized a feast on 8 June 1794.
- His last known words were 'Merci, monsieur', spoken to someone who gave him a handkerchief to wipe the blood from the bullet wound on his face.
- In popular culture, the excesses of the French Revolution are inextricably tied to the frightening image of the guillotine. According to historical records, around 2,639 people were guillotined in Paris during the nine months between autumn 1793 and summer 1794, much lesser than popular estimates, sometimes touching 40,000. Incredibly, the instrument was actually designed by a French physician named Joseph-Ignace Guillotin as a quicker, more painless method of capital punishment as compared to hanging or being killed by the sword that was common in eighteenth-century France.
- The guillotine remained the only legal method of execution in France until President François Mitterrand finally abolished the death penalty in 1981.

4. Simón Bolívar

Shouts of 'El Libertador' still echoed in his ears, but the tall, slender man with piercing black eyes was deep in thought. The intensity of the counter-revolutionary violence had horrified even this seasoned soldier's conscience. But still he proclaimed, 'Our tolerance is now exhausted... The war will be to the death.' This was Simón Bolívar, the Liberator — the legendary Venezuelan leader who had driven a series of revolutions across the northern part of South America during the early decades of the nineteenth century for freedom from Spanish rule. Eventually, he went on to become a respected statesman, the president of Peru and even had a newly-liberated country — Bolivia — named after him.

Early Life

Bolívar was born on 24 July 1783 into an aristocratic family of Caracas, Venezuela. Both his parents died early, and young Bolívar was brought up by his uncle with all the privileges of education and wealth. The boy was especially influenced by a tutor named Simón Rodríguez who was an avid reader of Jean-Jacques Rousseau's works. Through him, young Bolívar was introduced to the world of eighteenth-century liberal ideas on politics and philosophy.

In the manner of colonial families of means, at sixteen years of age, Bolívar was sent to Europe to complete his education. Three years later, he returned to his homeland not only as an accomplished young man but with a bride as well. In a tragic turn of events, Bolívar's young wife died of yellow fever within a year of their return to Venezuela. Heartbroken, Bolívar threw himself into the study of politics and soon was on his way to the nerve-centre of all revolutionary activities in Europe at the time—Paris.

Formative Years

Arriving in 1804 at the French capital, Bolívar met his old tutor and friend, Rodríguez, who introduced him to the throbbing intellectual life of Paris. Here, the young Venezuelan was quickly drawn into the rich matrix of political ideas and theories. Apart from rediscovering Rousseau, Bolívar also started reading Locke, Hobbes, Montesquieu, Leclerc and Voltaire. With all these new political philosophies churning in his mind, a meeting that

Bolívar had with a German naturalist known as Alexander von Humboldt left a particularly strong impression on him. Humboldt had recently returned from a tour of Hispanic America and told Bolívar that he thought its people were ready for self-governance. Bolívar now began examining his ideas about his homeland in a new light, and especially pondered long and deep during a journey to Rome that he took with Rodríguez. There, in an epiphanic moment at Mount Sacro, Bolívar recognized what he wanted to do with his life, and, with Rodríguez as witness, undertook an oath of liberating his country from Spanish rule.

Yet another definitive moment that went into the making of Bolívar as a revolutionary was his witnessing Napoleon's coronation as the emperor of France in 1804. It was a complex experience and left a deep impact—on one hand Bolívar was undoubtedly awed by the French general's sheer force of personality, ambition and strategic skills, while on the other, the institutionalized fawning on Bonaparte made him certain that he never wanted anything like that thrust on himself. Bolívar, fresh from his study of liberal political philosophy, was pained at the failure of all genuine revolutionary ideals evident in France's transformation into a monarchy.

Bolívar decided to return to his homeland, but not before visiting another recent site of a victorious revolutionary war—America. Colonial political forces under military leaders like George Washington, Nathanael Greene,

Benedict Arnold and others had defeated the British Crown's armies to form a new country. Indeed, at the time of Bolívar's arrival, the US was being governed by their first president, George Washington, according to their own constitution which had been formally accepted by the Congress in 1776.

Colonial Exploitation of South America

Within a few centuries of the Old World's discovery of South America, the Spanish Crown had established itself as the main colonial ruler. This inevitably led to extreme economic and social exploitation. While the Spanish government looted the continent of its natural wealth, like gold, silver, cocoa, grains, indigo and cattle, it flooded the colonial markets with highly-priced imports and heavy taxes. Spanish companies exercised trading monopolies, leading to the destruction of the local economy. Compounding this economic injustice was discrimination in all aspects of governance — all high-ranking posts in the bureaucracy and the military were reserved for Spanish officers. Then, there was the racial discrimination in all social dealings, with Spaniards ill-treating South American people. In general, all the colonial classes suffered — from the heavily-taxed wealthy landowners to traders, farmers, cattle hands and those who lived in the remotest parts of the jungles. The gold and profits thus looted by the

Spanish government went into the royal coffers to fund further colonizing voyages and invasions.

Spain, however, was dealt a rude blow by Bonaparte in 1805 when he invaded the Iberian Peninsula, disposed of the Spanish king and placed his own brother on the throne. With the royal administration brought down to its knees in Spain, a few far-thinking leaders in South America saw their chance to throw off the colonial yoke. Francisco de Miranda was among the first of such visionaries, and as early as 1806, had tried to liberate his country, almost single-handedly. But his campaign had proved unsuccessful, and he had to leave the continent.

By the time Bolívar became active, the timing was better, and he was able to convince like-minded people to come together to topple the Spanish administration. On 19 April 1810, the Spanish governor of Venezuela officially surrendered his powers and was expelled from the country. In May 1810, the local militia at Buenos Aires seized power. With a provisional government holding fort at Caracas, Bolívar left for England to raise support in the form of men, arms, money and the official recognition of Venezuela's independence. Though his expedition was not materially successful, he came back with useful knowledge of British forms of democratic government—more importantly, he got de Miranda to return with him to Venezuela.

Revolutionary Wars

After much deliberation, Venezuela's National Congress that had been formed to draft a new constitution finally declared independence on 5 July 1811. This was the founding of the First Republic. However, growing conflicts among its leaders offered the Spanish army an opportunity to get back power. De Miranda was defeated and imprisoned — regrettably with the aid of Bolívar and others.

However, Bolívar was not ready to surrender his dreams of Venezuela's liberation just yet. He managed to leave for New Granada, and once in Cartagena, he wrote his first major political tract tilted *The Cartagena Manifesto* or *El Manifiesto de Cartagena*. In this, he ascribed the failure of the First Republic to the lack of a strong, central leadership capable of rallying disparate opinions and interests, and if need be, overriding internal dissent. This was exactly what another military leader from the southern part of the continent — Argentina — had done. José de San Martin had managed to convince the local militias to give up their parochialism in favour of a common goal — to drive the Spanish rulers out. For this purpose, Martin had raised a revolutionary army, known as the Army of the Andes, and ran it along strong, centralized lines.

Inspired by Martin's example, Bolívar made another pitch to free Venezuela in 1813, but failed again. He escaped to New Granada, and for a while participated in military conflicts in the region. Fast running out of support, Bolívar fled to Jamaica, and there, in exile, wrote his greatest political tract titled *Letter from Jamaica*. In this, he made an impassioned plea for international, especially British, support for the liberation movement in Venezuela. Most inspiring, however, was the address to the people of South America to rise above internal differences of region, race, class, economy and culture, to come together as a consortium of nations of Hispanic America. In place of Spanish rule, he proposed the system of a constitutional republic for countries gaining independence. For New Granada, his plans of the new government replicated the British model of an elected lower house, a hereditary upper house and a nominated president.

After spending three years in the Orinoco Basin, Bolívar finally saw an opportunity in the spring of 1819. Leading an army of barely 2,500 men, Bolívar braved flooded rivers and snow-capped passes to enter New Granada and mount a surprise attack on the royalist forces. Bolívar's military gamble paid off, and on 7 August 1819, his victory in the Battle of Boyacá proved to be the turning point in the revolutionary history of South America. Three days later, Bolívar entered Bogotá and set up a new government, of which he became the president and supreme military commander.

Bolívar's final ambition was freeing the northern part of South America from Spanish control. To this end, in

December 1819, he convinced legislators to announce the establishment of Gran Colombia, which then included Venezuela, Quito or present-day Ecuador as well as the three departments of New Granada—roughly equivalent to present-day Colombia and Panama.

To transform this declaration into a reality, Bolívar formulated an elaborate military plan. First, he negotiated with the Spanish general, Pablo Morillo, for a six-month armistice in Venezuela, which gave him enough time to build his forces. In June 1821, he marched one more time to Caracas, this time to stay. After freeing Venezuela, he moved to Ecuador where it took him and his trusted friend, Antonio José de Sucre, around a year to take the capital city of Quito.

Fight for Peru

With Gran Colombia free of Spanish occupation, Bolívar now decided to march towards Peru, which had long been a bastion of royalist forces. However, this time, San Martin, approaching from the southern part of the continent, was not only ready to meet Bolívar midway, but had even captured Lima from the Spanish forces.

At the Guayaquil Conference on 26 July 1822, the two greatest South American revolutionary leaders met in the port city of Guayaquil in Ecuador. They both agreed that their mutual goal was the eviction of Spanish forces from the whole of Peru. However, the conference ended with Bolívar assuming total command of colonial forces while San Martin decided to leave Lima. The Spanish armies, holed up in the Peruvian highlands, were routed by Bolívar's carefully-planned military strategies, and with the Spanish viceroy losing the Battle of Ayacucho on 9 December 1824, Bolívar's victory was complete. He became the dictator of Peru, and in April the following year, Upper Peru, too, was brought under his control. Bolívar was now at the peak of his power — indicated by the naming of this newly-liberated state, Bolivia.

Treaty of Alliances

With most of South America freed from Spanish occupation, Bolívar now turned to his final goal — that of creating a league of Hispanic American states. In 1826, he organized a conference in Panama, which was attended by representatives of Colombia, Peru, Central America and Mexico, who signed a treaty of alliance. Bolívar, however, had dreamt of wider participation by South American countries, and even planned a loose federal system with biannual assemblies, as well as a common navy and army. But due to the wide variations in racial, class, regional and cultural interests of the people across the continent, such an idea of the united states of Hispanic America proved a non-starter.

Death and Legacy

The internal pulls and pressures finally gave way to a civil war in Gran Colombia, and to tide it over, Bolívar declared himself the dictator and called for the meeting of a national convention in April 1828. The situation, however, continued to slide towards disintegration, and after numerous setbacks, including assassination attempts, Bolívar decided to go into exile in Europe. But just before setting sail, he received news that his long-time trusted lieutenant, Sucre, had been assassinated. Heartbroken, he retired to the estate of a Spanish settler near Santa Marta, Colombia, where he finally died of tuberculosis on 17 December 1830.

Towards the end of his life, Bolívar lamented the difficulty of uniting the continent into a single political entity in the manner of its northern neighbour. 'I am ashamed to admit it,' he said, 'but independence is the only benefit we have gained, at the cost of everything else.' Even then, it was primarily his unflagging courage, steely determination and personal charisma that kept the South American revolutionary fires burning through some of its darkest times. Today, Bolívar is mainly remembered as the liberator of the continent from Spanish occupation, since he helped five present-day countries—Venezuela, Panama, Ecuador, Bolivia and Peru—gain their independence.

Fascinating Facts

- Bolívar's full name was quite a mouthful—he was christened Simon José Antonio de la Santísima Trinidad Bolívar Palacios Ponte y Blanco!
- With his mother dying when he was still a child, Bolívar was cared for by a woman slave named Hipólita, whom he described as the only mother he had ever known.
- During the liberation of Ecuador in 1822, Bolívar met and fell in love with a woman revolutionary named Manuela Sáenz. Though she would eventually accompany him to Peru and later to the presidential palace in Bogotá, the two would not marry—mainly because of Bolívar's vow upon his wife's death to never marry again.

5. Rani Lakshmibai

'...A woman highly respected and esteemed and...fully capable of...assuming the reins of government in Jhansi'. This was how Major John Malcolm, senior political agent, described Rani Lakshmibai to Lord Dalhousie while conveying the news of her husband Raja Gangadhar Rao's death in 1853. Actually, Rani Lakshmibai would prove to be much more. She would end up putting a tough fight to the British forces in the Revolt of 1857, while the popular image of her riding a horse, with her adopted child tied to her back and sword in hand, would emerge as the symbol of the motherland fighting for her independence from intruders.

Early Life

Little is known about Rani Lakshmibai before her arrival in Jhansi, apart from the fact that she was born in Varanasi sometime in the year 1828, into a Brahmin family, and was called Manikarnika, Manu for short. Her father was Moropant Tambe, who enjoyed the status of advisor to the brother of the deposed Maratha Peshwa and then later formed part of the Peshwa's retinue. Her mother was Bhagirathi, who died when Manikarnika was very young.

Being raised in the court of the exiled Peshwa, and without a mother's influence, Manikarnika enjoyed a lifestyle unusual for girls of the time. Along with other boys of the court, she was trained in horse riding and sword fighting, besides being taught to read and write. The self-assurance and ability to hold her own among men, even foreigners, can be traced back to this unconventional upbringing, as well as the support of her father.

Arrival in Jhansi

Jhansi, located immediately south of Delhi, Agra and Gwalior, as well as leading into the Deccan, had always enjoyed a strategic and economic importance. The Grand Trunk Road located close by was an important trading route, and transit duties earned from here was an important source of revenue for Jhansi. As a result, the kingdom, for long, had been coveted by Marathas and Orcha rulers.

The arrival of the East India Company, a British trading company, added a far more lethal component to the mix. Initially the Company carried out commercial activities to the common advantage of both British merchants and Indian rulers. However, by the mid-1850s, it had turned into an administrative force, with the right to the land revenues of Indian princes and farmers, and often intervening in matters of succession in Indian states. In keeping with this, Jhansi Fort was occupied by British forces in 1839, and they set up Gangadhar Rao as the titular king. Despite having limited resources, the middle-aged king gradually started introducing policies to improve Jhansi's economy and security, to the extent that in 1843, Jhansi was returned to its ruler.

This was also when Raja Gangadhar Rao married for a second time and brought to Jhansi the fifteen-year-old Manikarnika as his queen, who was now renamed Rani Lakshmibai. However, Gangadhar Rao soon became ill, and while on his deathbed, adopted a five-year-old boy called Damodar Rao as his legal heir. Major Robert Ellis, the British political agent in Jhansi, as well as Captain Martin, the commander of the British forces stationed there, acted as witnesses to the adoption.

However, Lord Dalhousie, who had become the governor general of India in 1848, brought in a controversial policy, titled Doctrine of Lapse. While Indian kings had been following the age-old tradition of adopting heirs in case they did not have biological children, Dalhousie's policy now sought to stop this. According to the Doctrine of Lapse, adopted children would no longer be recognized as heirs to the throne, and upon the death of a king without a natural successor, the kingdom would become a British territory.

Rani Lakshmibai already knew about Nana Sahib—the adopted son of Maratha Peshwa Baji Rao II—who had been exiled due to the Doctrine of Lapse. Determined to avoid such a fate for her adopted son, she began talks with Major Ellis in December 1853 and sent petitions to Lord Dalhousie requesting Damodar Rao to be recognized as the legal heir to the throne of Jhansi. When her appeals were turned down, Rani Lakshmibai even hired the services of an Australian lawyer named John Lang who had at the time shot to fame for winning a case on behalf of an Indian client against the British.

All of Rani Lakshmibai's efforts came to naught, and Jhansi lapsed to the British in May 1854. This was followed by a hectic round of negotiations between Rani Lakshmibai and Lord Dalhousie's agent, Sir Robert Hamilton, with regard to the future of Jhansi and her own living arrangements. Soon it became clear that despite Rani Lakshmibai's earnest requests to be allowed to retain the governance of Jhansi and the standard of living she had been used to, the British authorities were in no mood to oblige.

Gathering Clouds of Revolt

The British insensitivity towards Rani Lakshmibai was only one of the many instances of the high-handedness it had come to display towards Indian rulers. Besides, the recent vehemence of Christian evangelists and British interference in local customs and religious practices had begun to anger both the Indian ruling elite as well as the populace. Things finally came to a head when, in March 1857, soldiers who had refused to bite cartridges of the newly introduced Enfield rifle were executed. These cartridges were rumoured to be greased with the fat of cows and pigs, hence abhorrent to both Hindu and Muslim faiths. The news spread westwards, and in May 1857, long-simmering resentment against British authoritarianism exploded in an attack on British officers and their families by Indian troops in the cantonment town of Meerut.

From there, the revolt spread to other segments of the Indian population and to other cities like Delhi and Kanpur. When the rebels came within striking distance of Jhansi, Rani Lakshmibai was initially alarmed, since her first thoughts were the protection of her kingdom and its people. Thus, contrary to the popular notion that Rani Lakshmibai readily joined the Revolt of 1857, historical records show that she repeatedly sought security for her people from the British government against the approaching rebels. Rani Lakshmibai's fears were soon justified during the Jokhun Bagh massacre in which British men, women and children were killed by rebel forces that had entered Jhansi. Finally, in early 1858, the fickleness of the British authorities became completely clear to her and she realized that she would have to depend on her own skeletal resources to protect Jhansi and her family. On the other hand, because of the Jokhun Bagh incident, the British government decided that Rani Lakshmibai had been complicit in the killings, and had to be vanquished.

Fight to the Last

In preparation for the coming war, Rani Lakshmibai began bolstering the defences of Jhansi Fort. Manufacture of ammunition was speeded up and huge amounts of ration were stocked within the fort. Sometime in March 1858 the siege of Jhansi began. Rani Lakshmibai's gunners bravely responded to the pounding of British artillery. For a time there was even hope that Tantia Tope and his rebel forces would come to the aid of Jhansi. But with the Maratha leader being held at the Betwa river by the British forces, Rani Lakshmibai was on her own. She fought valiantly, but the British soldiers under General Hugh Rose finally broke the siege on 3 April 1858 and entered the Jhansi Fort. Still determined not to give in, Rani Lakshmibai fled the city with her son on horseback, eventually meeting up in Kalpi with other rebel leaders like Tantia Tope and Rao Sahib, the nephew of Nana Sahib. Though they were defeated by the British forces, they managed to escape, and in a lightning strike, captured the Scindia fort at Gwalior.

While the rest of the rebel army celebrated their surprise victory at the fort, Rani Lakshmibai, with Damodar Rao and her remaining attendants, retired to the Phool Bagh sector of Gwalior. For the next few days, she spent time preparing for the inevitable assault by the British that she knew would come. On 17 June 1858, she was the first to meet the approaching men of the 8th Hussars, led by General Rose. In the ensuing fight, Rani Lakshmibai lost her life — according to eyewitness accounts — fighting hand-to-hand with the British soldiers. Rani Lakshmibai's body was never found by the British, for, immediately after she fell, her own soldiers must have hurriedly cremated it to prevent it from falling into enemy hands.

Legacy

Today, Rani Lakshmibai is venerated as one of the front-line figures of India's first war of independence. And though her death reinforced British rule in Jhansi, among the larger consequences of the Revolt of 1857 was the realization by the British rulers that Indian customs and traditions had to be respected. More importantly, the infamous Doctrine of Lapse was abandoned by the British government as state policy.

Incidentally, there were many women like Lakshmibai who valiantly rose up against British occupation. While some like Begum Hazrat Mahal of Lucknow and Azizun

Bai of Kanpur fought the soldiers with weapons, ordinary women called 'bhatiyarins' (meaning innkeepers) often played an important role in the Revolt, with planning and logistics. All these women—like Rani Lakshmibai of Jhansi—demand our perennial homage for rising against the might of the British guns in the Revolt of 1857.

Fascinating Facts

- Quite unusually for the times, Lakshmibai's father accompanied her to her husband's house after her marriage to Raja Gangadhar Rao.
- During the time of military preparations against the British forces, and while fighting, Rani Lakshmibai would always have a small bejewelled sword and two pistols tucked into her cummerbund.

6. Emmeline Pankhurst

For a brief moment, she closed her eyes. And then, she was ready to receive the verdict. The jury found her guilty of breaking the law, to which her response was, 'I have no sense of guilt. I feel I have done my duty.' This was Emmeline Pankhurst in 1905, being sentenced to three years of rigorous imprisonment that would go on to include periods of solitary confinement as well. All this for agitating to give the women of England their due—the right to vote—the same as the men of the country. In 1903, she founded the Women's Social and Political Union, which would become one of the most high-profile women's organizations working for female empowerment and equality. The suffragette movement which she spearheaded finally won its goal of women's equal electoral franchise in 1928—also the year Emmeline Pankhurst died.

Early Life

Born on 14 July 1858 as Emmeline Goulden in Manchester, England, the future activist was raised in the midst of liberal political thinking that supported anti-slavery and women's rights movements. Her father, Robert Goulden, was a wealthy self-made industrialist, while her mother Sophie was an early supporter of women's suffrage, or the right to vote. One of the significant moments of her childhood was attending a suffrage meeting with her mother to hear Lydia Becker, who was the secretary of the influential Manchester National Society for Women's Suffrage as well as a leading figure of the Victorian women's rights movement. The talk impacted young Emmeline, who was then in school, deeply, so much so that she came away from the meeting 'a conscious and confirmed' suffragist.

Emmeline's growing consciousness was evident, as she convinced her parents to send her to Paris for a liberal education rather than merely learning social skills in English boarding schools for girls, as was the norm at the time. From 1873 to 1878, she studied at École Normale de Neuilly, a pioneer institution in Europe for higher education for girls, where she learnt not just sewing and embroidery, but chemistry and bookkeeping as well, and returned home fluent in French.

Soon after returning to Manchester, Emmeline met Dr Richard Pankhurst, a lawyer and an activist, for ultraliberal and rather unpopular issues. Among the causes he supported were education for the working class, home rule for Ireland and even the radical notion of the abolition of monarchy. However, what attracted Emmeline to Richard was his determined support to the cause of equal voting rights for women. By the time they married in 1879, he was already in his mid-forties, while Emmeline was just twenty-one. The couple went on to have five children—three girls and two boys—of whom only the girls survived till adulthood.

Growing Activism

For a period, they were political activists in London, but beset by financial woes, the Pankhursts were compelled to return to Manchester. There, they became part of the newly formed Labour Party, and Emmeline Pankhurst began supervising the local workhouse and even succeeded in improving conditions there to a great extent.

In 1898, Richard Pankhurst died suddenly of a perforated ulcer, leaving his family deep in debt. Emmeline Pankhurst took on a job in the registrar's office, which gave her a steady source of income. Her involvement with the workhouse and then as a registrar gave her first-hand knowledge of the economic difficulties faced by women mainly because of highly discriminatory laws. The newly-passed Married Women's Property Act, 1882, for which her own husband had tirelessly lobbied, had somewhat improved conditions, since, unlike before, women now had the right to inherit property and keep the money they earned after marriage. However, Emmeline Pankhurst realized that till the time women did not have a direct say in the making of laws, their condition could hardly be bettered. For this, women needed to have the power to send their representatives to parliament, and this could happen only when they had the right to vote.

Founding of Women's Social and Political Union

In order to organize and recharge the ongoing activism for women's suffrage, Emmeline Pankhurst founded the Women's Social and Political Union (WSPU) in 1903. This eventually became the fountainhead of a more militant movement that did not admit men as its members, and mainly reached out to working-class women. By now, two of her daughters, Christabel and Sylvia, had also joined the cause. Initially, derided as suffragettes by the press in comparison to the previous, more genteel suffragists, Emmeline Pankhurst's movement embraced the term, and even named their newspaper after it.

Again and again, the dominant political parties refused to make women's right to vote a priority. But each time, the suffragettes responded actively, staging protests, shouting slogans and going on hunger strikes. Even after they would be arrested, the activists would refuse to pay fines, and instead, choose to go to prison. Emmeline Pankhurst herself would be imprisoned several times, and on one occasion, her hunger strike resulted in violent force-feeding by the authorities. In 1908, she organized the largest-ever political rally in the history of London in which around 5,00,000 people turned up at Hyde Park for a WSPU demonstration.

As the suffragette movement swelled in strength and numbers, the government, instead of opening negotiations, responded even more harshly. In 1913, it passed the infamous Temporary Discharge for Ill Health Act. Criticized as the Cat and Mouse Act, it empowered law enforcement officials to release prisoners on hunger strike, and when they became healthier, the activists were arrested again. This led to even more violent protests, in the form of arson and bombings. In one of the most alarming responses, WSPU member Emily Davison threw herself under the king's horse at Derby and died. The incident led several members of WSPU to reject Emmeline Pankhurst's leadership, and among the dissidents was her own daughter, Sylvia.

War Effort and Death

With the outbreak of World War I, the suffragette movement suspended its militant tactics and instead reached a truce with the government. The WSPU agreed to support the war efforts, and in return, its imprisoned members were released. Despite her advanced age and failing health, Emmeline Pankhurst herself dived into war relief—helping orphans and destitute women, besides taking on hectic speaking tours to the US and Russia. Her tireless lobbying eventually helped the government and people at large to recognize women's contribution to society at a time when the majority of able-bodied men were at the front lines. All these efforts paved the way for the Representation of the People Act on 6 February 1918, according to which the parliament granted voting rights to all women over thirty. Ten years later, it was extended to all women over twenty-one years of age, the same as for men. Unfortunately, Emmeline Pankhurst did not live to see the final achievement of the suffragette movement as she passed away only weeks earlier, on 14 June 1928.

Legacy

While Emmeline Pankhurst is now forever enshrined as the chief figure of the suffragette movement, many forget her untiring efforts at improving the conditions of workhouses, destitute women and orphaned children. Most importantly, she recognized the direct link between women's socio-economic disabilities and their disenfranchised state, which guided later feminists across the world to demand political representation. Despite criticism of her militant methods from various sections of society, including her own organization and family, Emmeline Pankhurst never doubted the seriousness of the need to win voting rights for women and be at par with men—a position made famous by her quote, 'We are here not because we are lawbreakers; we are here in our efforts to become lawmakers.'

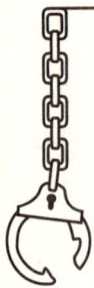

Fascinating Facts

- During her engagement with Dr Richard Pankhurst, Emmeline had actually suggested that they first live in a state of free union (what is now understood as a live-in relationship) in order to check their compatibility.
- As she was away from England during her husband's final illness, Emmeline Pankhurst learnt about his death from a newspaper article.
- During the war, she adopted four orphans, and when asked how she would bring them up at fifty-seven, and without any steady income, she replied, 'My dear, I wonder I didn't take forty.'

7. Mahatma Gandhi

Hands and fingers moving in rhythm to the spinning wheel of the charkha, he felt the familiar movement calm his soul. Painful memories of the recent violence seemed to ebb a little, and the late afternoon winter sun appeared to shine a bit warmer. It was time to head for the prayer meeting at the Birla House—Gandhi rose and walked out.

The same setting sun would also witness the end of a life chiefly responsible for leading the non-violent nationalist movement of India against British rule. A revolutionary of a different kind, Gandhi's weapons of non-cooperation and civil disobedience would later be used by leaders in different places of the world, and forever enshrine him in India as the Father of the Nation.

Early Life

Born as Mohandas Karamchand Gandhi on 2 October 1869 in Porbandar, Gujarat, the future Indian leader was raised according to the strict ethos of an upper-caste Hindu Gujarati family with a strong bent towards Jainism. Non-vegetarianism, unwavering obedience to elders, fasting, and non-violence towards all creatures were instilled in him by a deeply religious mother. However, Gandhi's father was the dewan or chief minister of the then royal principality of Porbandar, who was responsible for its day-to-day governance. Young Gandhi would probably imbibe administrative skills and the art of getting people with varied priorities and expectations to work together from him.

At school, Gandhi proved to be a mediocre student. With his father's move from Porbandar to Rajkot, educational opportunities improved for Gandhi, but he remained a shy child in school. He would perform fairly well in studies, but would run back home as soon as school ended, to avoid having to talk to anyone. His schooling was interrupted for a year because of his marriage to a girl of the same age as him, thirteen, named Kasturba.

Today, perhaps, the most interesting aspect about Gandhi's young adulthood is his account of his secret religious transgressions, later detailed in the autobiographical *My Experiments with Truth*. Young

Mohandas flirted with atheism and indulged in petty thieving for a while. He smoked, but more scandalously for a boy brought up according to the strictest Hindu and Jain tenets, ate meat.

Eventually, this phase proved to be the stepping stone towards building a stronger character, marked by steely determination. Soon, he grew out of this secret rebellious phase and determined never to engage in acts forbidden by his faith—a promise that he kept ever since.

Becoming a Barrister

In accordance with cultural traditions, Gandhi deferred whenever his future was discussed by elders. His family proposed that he become a barrister, and was ready to sponsor his education in England for the purpose. Gandhi was at this time already enrolled in Samaldas College at Bhavnagar, but since he did not like it there, he readily agreed to go to England. This, in itself, was a major step in self-assertion, since, according to the conservative Hindu tenets, crossing the seas was akin to loss of faith. Gandhi pacified his mother by taking a vow to avoid wine, women and meat during his stay on foreign shores. Finally, in September 1888, he set sail for England.

In London, he joined the Inner Temple to study law, but found the overall change to western culture hard. Adapting to a cold climate, a western way of dressing and foreign ways of life proved challenging, and he was particularly troubled by the lack of vegetarian food. Eventually, though, he discovered a vegetarian restaurant, and his dietary concerns out of the way, Gandhi now embraced the cosmopolitanism of London. He joined the executive committee of the London Vegetarian Society and even contributed articles to its journal. Meeting more people through its conferences, Gandhi's social and intellectual horizons broadened—he was not only introduced to the Bible but also to the English translation of the Bhagavad Gita, a seminal text of his own religion that he had never read in India. In all, Gandhi's time in London brought him in touch with theosophical, anti-materialistic and humanitarian ideologies and movements that he would have never encountered in India, and which would go on to shape his world view in important ways.

Arrival in South Africa

Despite returning from England with a law degree, Gandhi found it difficult to get work in India. So, in 1893, he accepted a year's contract to work for an Indian law firm in Natal, South Africa.

Though he had been brought up in a land also colonized by the British, in South Africa, Gandhi felt the worst of the racial discrimination. The series of insults came to a head when, returning from Durban to Pretoria on an overnight train, he was thrown out of a first-class compartment and then beaten up by the white driver of a stagecoach because he would not give up his seat for a white traveller. This humiliation struck deep within Gandhi, who, all this while, had been diffident and wary of asserting himself. He now decided that he would not take any sort of injustice lying down.

It was this new conviction that compelled Gandhi to stay back even after his annual contract in Natal was over. In July 1894, he started campaigning against a proposal of the Natal Legislative Assembly which would take away the right of Indian settlers to vote. Though Gandhi could not prevent the passage of the bill, his efforts resulted in unifying the scattered Indian community, and in turning international attention to the unjust discriminations under which Indians were living in South Africa.

Growing Political Resistance

After a brief visit to India in 1896, Gandhi returned to South Africa and gave its British rulers a visible lesson in non-partisan living. Despite the discrimination faced, Gandhi rallied support in favour of the British cause in the Boer War and raised a 1,100-strong ambulance corps.

However, rather than giving any evidence of just governance, the British government responded with a highly discriminatory proposal of compulsory registration for Indian settlers. Gandhi decided to oppose this, and on 11 September 1906, organized a mass protest meeting at the Empire Theatre in Johannesburg. There, the Indian supporters pledged to resist the harsh law with non-violent methods, becoming the first example of Gandhi's doctrine of satyagraha or devotion to truth. For the next seven years, thousands of Indians went on strike or gave up British associations, facing, in exchange, harsh punishment, ranging from loss of livelihood to imprisonment, flogging and even firing. At the same time, Gandhi also put his ideals of socio-economic reform into action by heading two farms in which men and women of all castes and religions were welcome to live and work together. When, in 1913, state brutality perpetrated against non-violent Indians got wide negative publicity across world, the colonial government was forced to open negotiations with Gandhi.

Though the settlement did not provide a long-term solution to Indian settlers' problems in South Africa, it marked a new maturing of Gandhi's quest. He now decided to fight the same battle with the same weapons in his homeland. Though, during World War I, he refused to engage openly with the British colonial government, the latter's insistence on pushing the Rowlatt Act compelled Gandhi to intervene. According to this highly oppressive law, Indians could be jailed without trial under charges of sedition.

Leader of the Masses

In the spring of 1919, Gandhi launched his satyagraha against the Rowlatt Act. Gandhi now took to travelling across India, raising awareness not only against unjust British policies but also against regressive social customs. For the first time, people came together in numbers never before witnessed in the history of the Indian subcontinent. British panic spilled over in the act of utmost brutality when, on 13 April 1919, British soldiers showered bullets on a peaceful prayer meeting held in Jallianwala Bagh, Amritsar, killing 400 people, including women and children.

Gandhi drew on the nationwide sentiments of horror and outrage and unified them into nationalist agitation using non-violent methods like strikes, peaceful marches and prayer meetings. Not surprisingly, he was invited to lead the Indian National Congress (INC) in 1921, transforming the party from a club of elite Indians to a grass-roots political organization. Gandhi's non-cooperation movement inspired supporters to boycott British institutions like schools, colleges and courts, as well as British goods. Even more importantly, it brought Hindus and Muslims together against the common enemy, the British government. However, at the height of the non-cooperation movement, Gandhi decided to call it off, in response to the British force used against a peaceful march of peasants in Chauri Chaura, Bihar.

The rising tide of nationalism petered out and Gandhi himself was imprisoned. Upon his release in February 1924, Gandhi found the Congress in disarray as well as Hindu-Muslim unity in jeopardy. Despite being elected president of the INC, Gandhi could not create much of an impact on the political landscape.

But all that changed when the British formed a constitutional reform commission for India under Sir John Simon without including a single Indian. This blatant injustice breathed new fire into nationalist feelings in Indians, and once again, Gandhi took charge of the non-violent movement against British rulers. The high point of this phase was the Salt March of March 1930 to protest the tax levied on the most basic item of use, salt. The march symbolized opposition to the colonial might by even the poorest sections of Indians, who courted imprisonment in thousands.

With the failure of the Round Table Conference of 1931, the British government turned on the repression against Gandhi's supporters in India. He was imprisoned, and in an attempt to divide Indians, the government offered separate electorates to the lowest section of Indian society, then termed 'untouchables'. To protest this policy of division, Gandhi undertook a fast, which not only compelled all stakeholders to effect a compromise, but more importantly, made Indians aware of the evil of this highly discriminatory practice in their own society.

Increasingly, Gandhi distanced himself from active politics and focused on propagating socio-economic reforms suited to the predominantly agrarian populace of India.

With the outbreak of World War II, Indian leaders offered their support to Britain in return for complete freedom once the war was over. However, continuing British equivocation on the matter of independence, and worse, colonial efforts to sow discord between Hindus and Muslims angered Gandhi, and he launched the Quit India Movement in 1942. Unlike his previous call for satyagraha, this time, Gandhi demanded the removal of British rulers by any means necessary. The British government came down hard on Indians, and with the imprisonment of Gandhi and core leaders of the movement, it died out.

A Costly Freedom

The 1945 victory of the Labour Party in Britain brought about a change in the political attitude, and negotiations regarding the transfer of power to Indians began. However, increasingly strident demands by Muhammad Ali Jinnah of the Muslim League for a separate nation for Muslims led to new difficulties. In the end, with spreading communal riots, the three sides agreed to the Mountbatten Plan of 1947, under which two new dominions of India and Pakistan would be formed in mid-August, 1947.

Gandhi was distraught at the partition of the country

and was determined to withdraw from public life. However, the horrors of unprecedented Hindu-Muslim riots forced him to return to the limelight. He called for peace, and twice went on a fast, demanding people of both faiths to come to their senses. Though he achieved some measure of success in stemming the tide of communal violence, especially in Calcutta in September 1947 and in Delhi in January 1948, he failed to convince everyone. On 30 January 1948, while going to a prayer meeting, Gandhi was shot and killed by a Hindu bigot, Nathuram Godse.

Legacy

Like the times he lived through, Gandhi's legacy passed through highs and lows. On one hand, he was hailed as the 'Father of the Nation' and venerated as the 'Mahatma', while, on the other, he was criticized for timidity by Indian political extremists and for a Hindu-biased vision of future India by Muslim leaders. The later Dalit movement pointed out his half-hearted measures against the caste system while feminists have picked out misogynistic strands from his spiritual ideals.

For all such critiques of Gandhi, there is little doubt about him being just the leader India needed in its darkest hour of colonial repression. Gandhi realized that Indian manpower could never match the might of British firepower; instead, the sheer magnitude of the Indian population and its spiritual courage could be mobilized into overwhelming and shaming the British rulers into realizing that their lofty philosophies of equality and liberty of man should be applied to all. Gandhi's legacy of non-violent agitation was later visible in action in the 1960s in America as Martin Luther King Jr led the Civil Rights Movement, as well as in South Africa as Nelson Mandela demanded an end to apartheid.

In 2007, Gandhi's birthday was declared by the United Nations (UN) as the International Day of Non-violence to honour the great leader for his methods and ideals embodied in the doctrine of satyagraha.

Fascinating Facts

- Gandhi was referred to by the title of Mahatma, meaning 'Great Soul', but he once said that 'the woes of the Mahatmas are known only to the Mahatmas'.
- During the course of his life, Gandhi was the target of six known assassination attempts.

8. Vladimir Lenin

After the momentous events of 7 November 1917, the Kremlin courtyard seemed uncanny in its silence. The sky was freezing in the cold — winter was already here. The snow crunched as two men walked past a large cannon and two cannon balls — these were Vladimir Dmitriyevich Bonch-Bruyevich and Vladimir Lenin, the former being the latter's secretary. Lenin would eventually be remembered as one of the greatest revolutionaries of the twentieth century.

Lenin had spearheaded the Russian Revolution of 1917 which had ended the reign of the Tsars in Russia and replaced monarchy with a socialist rule in one of the largest countries of the world. His ideology, which later came to be known as Leninism, was a combination of Marxism and communism. It went on to become widely influential, inspiring countless socialist movements around the world.

VLADIMIR LENIN

Early Life

Born as Vladimir Ilyich Ulyanov on 22 April 1870 in Simbirsk, Russia, Lenin grew up in a well-educated middle-class family. While his father had a Mongol heritage and could lay some claim to the lower end of hereditary nobility, Lenin's mother had Jewish antecedents. Lenin's father started out as a schoolteacher, but eventually achieved social standing as an inspector of schools. More importantly, the family was a fertile ground for liberal ideas. Except one sibling who did not survive till adulthood, Lenin and his four siblings turned out to be involved—in some capacity or the other—with the revolutionary forces of the times.

Young Lenin was a good student with a special aptitude for the classical languages, who went on to stand first in his high school exams. However, the increasing intolerance of the tsarist regime cast a long shadow on his childhood. In fact, Lenin's father came under a great deal of stress towards the end of his life, since public education was seen as an important channel of disseminating revolutionary ideas. He died in 1866, but what followed was a greater blow to young Lenin—the arrest of his elder brother Alexander for revolutionary activities against the government. The group that Alexander was part of was charged with plotting the murder of Tsar Alexander III, and along with other members, Lenin's brother, too, was executed in 1867. These two incidents turned Lenin squarely against the tsarist rule, and he became even more determined to end the monarchy in Russia.

Political Education

To further his goal, Lenin decided to study law, and he enrolled at the Kazan University in 1887. But his involvement in an anti-government students' march led to his suspension in the very first year of college. He then decided to head for the village of Kokushkino where his grandfather had an estate. Here, he met up with his sister Anna—another revolutionary trying to keep a low profile. The siblings spent their days reading books and treatises by other revolutionary figures, and discussing their theories.

Lenin was especially influenced by Karl Marx whose *Das Kapital* presents a heavy indictment of the capitalist system in economics as well as in politics, religion and relationships. Marx proposed a model of a classless economy where all would be equal, and it was this idea that shaped Lenin's own ideology. At the same time, he realized that the unique conditions of Russia meant any revolution would have to address the problems of the land, and to this end he was greatly influenced by thinkers like Bakunin. Yet another important work that Lenin came across at this time was the Russian novel

What Is to Be Done? by Nikolay Chernyshevsky, which revolves around a fiery revolutionary character named Rakhmetov.

After returning to Kazav, Lenin shocked everybody by securing a first-class degree in his law exams — without having attended classes or having received any kind of help from any teacher or even a student. With his family having moved to Samara, Lenin, too, began practising law there and often helped poor Russian peasants in their fight against a legal system that was heavily weighted in favour of the ruling classes.

Active Politics

Lenin realized that for a more active involvement he needed to be at the heart of the political regime, which was then the capital, St. Petersburg. Here, he soon became involved in revolutionary activities, and as a result, was arrested and banished to Siberia along with his fiancée Nadezhda Krupskaya for as long as three years. In exile, Lenin married Nadezhda, and the couple set up a home as well as they could.

After his political exile, Lenin travelled across Europe to gain first-hand knowledge of other revolutionary activities. In Munich, he even started a newspaper, *Iskra*, so that both Russian and European traditions of Marxism could nurture each other and bring about wider changes in the world. In his own homeland, the political situation was fast deteriorating, and he returned to Russia to attend the Second Congress of the Russian Social Democratic Labour Party in 1903. Here he found himself pitted against another leader, Julius Martov, whose group of supporters were known as Mensheviks, a group that advocated a more gradual process of political reorganization. Lenin, on the other hand, pitched for more disciplined and involved party leadership that would be able to better organize, enlist and enthuse the party workers on the ground. 'Give us an organization of revolutionaries,' Lenin said in his hallmark address, 'and we will overturn Russia!' Not surprisingly, the Mensheviks were sidelined by Lenin and his comrades who were known as Bolsheviks.

Russia's defeat in the Russo-Japanese War had not only left the economy in shambles but had revealed the complete disconnect between the tsarist regime and the people. The final straw proved to be the 1905 St. Petersburg firing in which the Tsar's security opened fire on a group of unarmed workers who had arrived at the city palace to submit a petition for fair working conditions to Emperor Nicholas II. The incident left hundreds dead, and many more injured. The event shook the monarchy enough to introduce some political reforms — the most significant of which was the creation of the Duma, which would be Russia's first elected legislative assembly.

The Russian Revolution

However, all this was too little, too late. The growing discontent of the Russian people was obvious, and Lenin believed this was the right time to push for a total change in the political system of the country. However, once again, he found his plans opposed by Martov and his Mensheviks who were in favour of the rise of the bourgeoisie (middle-class people). Lenin, on the other hand, was determined in his support of the proletariat (working-class people). The conflict between the two revolutionary leaders came to a head in 1912, when the Russian Social-Democratic Workers' Party (RSDWP) split into two groups and Lenin organized his own Bolshevik Congress.

Soon, though, Europe was in the grip of a larger force, and in 1914, World War I broke out in the continent. Lenin saw in this an opportunity to usher in Russia's own political transformation, but the time was not right. He decided to live in neutral Switzerland during the war and occupy himself with his writing. The result was one of his most influential works, *Imperialism: The Highest Stage of Capitalism*, in which he argued that worldwide capitalism would inevitably end in wars of the most terrifying intensity and widest possible scale.

Though Lenin had been frustrated in his revolutionary plans in 1914, the fire that his vision had lit among Russians had not been completely put out by the clouds of World War I. Indeed, by 1917, its people had had enough of violence and financial hardships. They blamed the tsarist regime for their numerous ills, and as a result, the monarchy was deposed, and in its place, a provisional government was set up.

Lenin arrived in the midst of these events and quickly took charge of what came to be known as the October Revolution. He started by deposing the provincial government that he accused of serving only bourgeoisie interests; instead, he rallied his Bolsheviks to fight for the proletariat that would place workers, peasants and soldiers in power. The result was the creation of the Union of Soviet Socialist Republics, or the USSR. In order to bring about the widest possible transformation, Lenin ordered the closure of several traditional government institutions, and in their place, established ruling mechanisms which answered directly to him. In this way, he started securing his own power in the USSR, of which he was now the de facto ruler.

Civil War

No bid to power could go unchallenged, of course. Opposed to Lenin and his supporters — now known as the Red forces — were many of the former tsarist generals, admirals and other monarchist supporters, termed the White forces. This led to a three-year-long civil war from

1918 to 1920 during which the White forces were helped by the Allied powers of World War I in the form of troops and arms. This was because a communist regime in Russia was contrary to the interests of Allied countries like the US and Britain.

In 1918, there was a bid on Lenin's life, and he was shot thrice. Though he survived the attack, he became exceedingly suspicious and more reactionary than ever. What followed was one of the most violent episodes of political repression in the history of the modern world, termed the Red Terror. Hundreds of people were arrested, shot and executed on mere suspicion of them being supporters of the White forces. He ordered the setting-up of show trials and concentration camps to strike fear into the heart of anyone who would dare challenge his authority. In this way, he managed to eliminate not only his political rivals, but any hint of political opposition. Lastly, as the final proof of his exalted position, all forms of religion and public worship were outlawed.

Rebuilding the Nation

Despite all his excesses, Lenin was too much of a leader to know that violence alone could not be used to secure his position. Long periods of breakdown in law and order were now making the economic consequences felt. Food and industrial production had plunged to abysmal depths.

Famine and poverty were rife in society. Indeed, in 1921, Lenin was faced with the same discontent in the form of peasant revolts and urban strikes that had led to the Revolution. He thus turned his attention to bettering the economic conditions of the people and addressing the need for food, livelihood and financial well-being. This took the form of the New Economic Policy whereby farmers were allowed to sell their grain in the open market. In this way, Lenin achieved a compromise between his earlier hardcore communism and free economic policy to avoid a total economic collapse of the country.

Final Years and Death

Years of mental and physical stress had taken their toll on Lenin—evidence of this was a series of strokes that he suffered between 1922 and 1924. As a result, he was unable to speak again and was left partially paralysed. However, Lenin continued to write, and with his remaining strength, managed to put together a treatise of sorts that later came to be known as *The Testament*. This was his comment on the political situation of the country at that time, which was marked by the rise of a new leader on the Soviet horizon—Joseph Stalin. He had become the general secretary of the Communist Party, and in order to safeguard his power, had restricted all access to Lenin who still held considerable sway in the government and among the people of the USSR. After Lenin's second stroke, Stalin even tried to prevent him from accessing any information on what was happening in the country. As a result, in *The Testament*, Lenin came down severely on Stalin's naked push for dictatorial power and warned of the consequences for his beloved Soviet Russia.

Ten months after suffering a third stroke, Lenin passed away on 21 January 1924 in the village now known as Gorki Leninskiye.

Legacy

Lenin and his leadership during the Russian Revolution was the most spectacular victory of the power of the people in the world. The sheer size of Russia and its population made communism's victory in the country a watershed episode of world history. The new era prophesied by Marx had arrived, and despite the eventual economic confusion, Lenin was upheld as the figure who could guide other downtrodden people and societies into a new age of equality.

Fascinating Facts

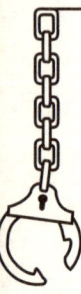

- As part of the Red Terror, Lenin founded a secret police known as the Cheka to identify and destroy his political rivals overnight. Lenin also engineered the complete destruction of a class called the Kulaks.
- In one infamous instance of the Red Terror, Lenin ordered his followers to kill as many members of the church as possible.
- In his later years, Lenin was so depressed by the state of his own health that he tried to commit suicide by taking poison several times, though unsuccessfully.
- After Lenin's death, his body was embalmed and placed in a mausoleum on Moscow's Red Square for all to see.

9. Mao Zedong

The fourteen-year-old boy stood alone in the paddy field and seethed in anger. His father's rebuke was still ringing in his ears. As if being pulled out from school was not enough, now his family was planning to tie him down to the life of a householder. He threw a glance at his home beyond the lush fields—one day he would leave this village, he thought. He could feel it inside his bones—he was meant to belong to not just one family or village, but to all of China. The boy would eventually go on to become the most powerful leader of twentieth-century China—Mao Zedong. He would not only head the Chinese Communist Party from 1935 till his death, but also serve as the chairman of the People's Republic of China from 1949 to 1959. During this time, he would lead the Cultural Revolution in China, bringing about the widest social, political and economic transformation in the most populous country on earth.

Early Life

Mao was born on 26 December 1893 at Shaoshan, in the Chinese province of Hunan. While other farmers in his village often faced economic difficulties, Mao's father was a grain trader, therefore, his family was better off than most. But even though he grew up in relative comfort, as a boy, Mao often found himself at odds with his strict authoritarian father. Mao's mother, on the other hand, was a loving and supportive person.

In keeping with the social traditions of the time, as Mao turned fourteen, his marriage was arranged. He was already frustrated at having to leave school in order to work on the family farms, but the prospect of being married off to a person he did not know roused the seeds of rebellion in young Mao. He rejected the marriage proposal, and as soon as he turned seventeen, decided to leave his village to go to Changsha, the capital of Hunan province. There, he got himself admitted to a secondary school and continued his education.

Political Beginnings

A wider exposure to a social and cultural life brought in its wake a greater political consciousness in Mao. He began to reflect on the centuries of economic and social exploitation that the monarchy had wrought on the common people of China. The farmers, labourers and other people who made up the working class slogged day and night, but their economic condition remained miserable for generations. As they sank deeper into decadence and incompetence, the privileged royalty and aristocracy, on the other hand, remained oblivious to the sufferings of the subjects.

Seeking to make a difference in some way, Mao joined Kuomintang, the Nationalist Party. His chance came in 1911 when the Chinese statesman Sun Yat-sen led the Xinhai Revolution, which deposed the monarchy in China, and in its place established the Republic of China. In the new order of things, Mao decided to further his education and started studying for a teaching degree that he obtained in 1918. With news of his mother's death, there was nothing more to take him back to his village. So, he decided to make his way to the capital city, Beijing.

Instead of the teaching job that Mao had hoped to get there, he had to settle for the post of a librarian's assistant at Beijing University. However, the trade-off did not turn out to be too bad, since his work continued to provide him access to books and the world of ideas, besides allowing him to attend a few classes in his spare time. Thus, he became aware of the Russian Revolution which had replaced a centuries-old monarchical system with communism in the USSR. Mao began dreaming of a similar change for China where a new political, social and economic order would bring an end to wide-ranging inequalities that generations of Chinese had been suffering.

To this end, Mao began rethinking his political allegiances. Though the Kuomintang Party had replaced the monarchy, it had not been able to overhaul the entire social system. Instead, he found himself increasingly attracted to Lenin's ideology, which called for the complete abolition of the class system. As such, in 1921, Mao, along with some other activists, established the Chinese Communist Party (CCP). He began to work to uplift the conditions of the peasantry, which was among the most oppressed classes in China. The work done by members of the CCP went down well among the masses, and membership of the party began to swell. National leaders like Yat-sen realized that it would be imprudent to stand in the way of popular opinion, and ordered Kuomintang workers to follow a policy of cooperation with the CCP. It was then only a matter of time before Mao quickly rose through the rungs of the CCP—from one of its founders and then as an assemblyman delegate, he was invited to be part of the central executive committee of the Shanghai branch of the party.

Crossing Swords with Kuomintang

The peaceful coexistence with Kuomintang ended with the death of Chinese president Yat-sen in March 1925. The succession of Chiang Kai-shek ushered in a hardening of opposition to the CCP. Personally too, Kai-shek was more orthodox and authoritarian. He was suspicious of Mao's growing influence in Chinese national politics and was determined to do his utmost to stop it. One of the ways was the dreaded purge of 1927 in which thousands of communists, and even casual supporters, were picked up by Kai-shek's forces without any legal process and imprisoned, or even killed.

Initially, Mao tried to fight back by putting together an army of peasants, but they were outnumbered by Kai-shek's armies. After fleeing to the highlands of Jiangxi Province, Mao and his supporters started regrouping themselves. Since Kai-shek's forces found it difficult to patrol the hilly terrain regularly, Mao established a provincial government in Jiangxi. He also trained his supporters in guerrilla tactics, which often mounted costly attacks on Kai-shek's soldiers. Like other authoritarians, though, Mao, around this time, began showing signs of growing dictatorship. Increasingly, he began to meet any sign of political opposition with harsh punishment that included imprisonment, torture and then execution.

By 1934, the writ of Mao's communist republic was running in around ten provinces in Jiangxi. Kai-shek realized that the only way to stop his growing influence was to mount a full-scale attack on the communist base. With this in mind, Kai-shek ordered almost one million government forces, in October 1934, to surround Mao's stronghold. Even as other communist leaders debated on how to meet this challenge, Mao decided on the most prudent option—retreat.

Long Walk to Freedom

For the next twelve long months, around 1,00,000 communist members and their families uprooted themselves from the Jianxi province to march northwards and westwards where they could be safe from the marauding Kuomintang soldiers. This event has gone down in history as the Long March, during the course of which Chinese communist workers and supporters covered around 8,000 miles, braving physical hazards such as icy mountains and marshy swamps. Not surprisingly, out of the original 1,00,000 who set out from Jiangxi, only 30,000 managed to arrive to relative safety at Yan'an, in northern China.

Though the Long March had proved to be costly in terms of human life, it passed into folklore as the journey of deliverance. Ordinary people across China now began looking upon Yan'an as the destination of freedom, and many decided to act upon it too. Most importantly, it further widened Mao's reputation in China as the true leader who could change things for the better.

Mao's opportunity came in July 1937 with Japanese invasion of the eastern Chinese territory. The Kuomintang soldiers suffered one defeat after another, which put Kai-shek in danger of losing political authority. Desperate for any type of support, Kai-shek reached out to Mao and promised the latter truce if the CCP would bring in reinforcement of men and arms. Mao agreed, and with some help from the Allied Powers who were opposed to the Axis Powers, Japan and Germany, drove out the Japanese invaders. The victory proved beyond doubt that Mao was now the most powerful leader in China. As Kai-shek and his remaining supporters fled to Taiwan to form a government in exile, Mao and his followers marched triumphantly into Beijing. On 1 October 1949, from the iconic Tiananmen Square in Beijing, Mao announced the birth of the People's Republic of China.

Introducing Reforms

Now that Mao was the unchallenged leader of China, he set about overhauling the traditional institutions of the country. Though the monarchy had already been abolished by Yat-sen, the long-entrenched class system had persisted in various forms. Mao now abolished all class privileges, and theoretically at least, declared China to be a classless society. Since the vast majority of ordinary Chinese people depended on agriculture, the first of his major reforms brought about land reorganization. Large estates belonging to the erstwhile nobility and warlords were taken over by the government and restructured into agricultural communes where the smaller farmers could work and receive fair returns of their labour.

Like other Oriental cultures, China was a staunchly patriarchal and traditional society. Mao now declared women to have the same legal status as men. More importantly, educational and work opportunities were opened to women after centuries of them being restricted to the domestic sphere. Also, education was made accessible to men of all classes, and healthcare was provided to all, leading to rise in literacy as well as life expectancy.

All these reforms had the biggest impact on the rural areas of China, where, for generations, the common people had been suffering from class inequality. In urban areas, however, Mao's reforms started generating discontent because of the strong-arm tactics, and at times, even explicit violence that they usually involved. Reading the mood on the ground, Mao launched the Hundred Flowers Campaign in 1956, which was intended to provide a democratic space to professionals, intellectuals and students in cities to debate issues and concerns. However, the intensity of people's objections and disapproval took even Mao by surprise, and the veteran leader responded with swift and harsh repression. Shrugging off all semblance of democracy, he ordered the arrest and even execution of hundreds of members of the urban civil society who dared to express dissent.

MAO ZEDONG

The Great Leap Forward

Though Mao's crackdown on the urban intelligentsia was brutal, it was nothing compared to the scale of destruction wrought by his ambitious economic policies, under what came to be touted as the Great Leap Forward. In his rush to impose communist economic policies, Mao had ordered small farmers to work in agricultural communes. Though theoretically equitable, the policy failed to take into account centuries of farming practices and culture. Above all, its coercive methods defeated any good intention that might have been there. Farmers were forced to give up whatever little land they possessed, and anyone who opposed was killed.

The consequences of such hasty, ill-conceived and harsh measures were not long in coming. They failed most spectacularly in the face of natural disasters like floods and bad harvests. When this continued for three years, food production practically came to a standstill, and China was hit by the worst famine in the modern era. Between 1959 and 1961, around forty million people died of starvation, and whole villages were wiped out, making this one of the worst man-made disasters in the history of the world. The enormity of human tragedy was cleverly obfuscated to the ordinary Chinese citizens and even the outside world. Exaggerated figures of industrial production continued to be parroted to the people of the country, weaving the fiction of the Great Leap Forward.

Historians still do not agree on whether Mao was aware of the real state of affairs in China. According to some sources, only very powerful communist party leaders knew what was actually happening, and they kept Mao in the dark about the scale of the tragedy. Whatever may have been the case, the result was that for the first time in his political career, Mao found himself sidelined in the CCP.

The Cultural Revolution

However, the wily old leader still had a trick or two up his sleeve, and he began planning his return to power. The relaunch was provided by the publication of his selected writings, titled *Quotations from Chairman Mao*. Soon, this handbook that had been compiled by a devoted supporter named Lin Biao became popular as the Little Red Book among all his supporters. Mao was back in the public gaze.

He continued with a few other publicity stunts like swimming in the Yangtze River in 1966, which was played up as the agelessness of the 75-year-old leader. But Mao's real intention was to drum up a national crisis to which he would provide a neat solution. This was kick-started by spreading rumours about a bourgeoisie plot to replace the communist government with the much-hated capitalist system. The rumours were directed at the contemporary young Chinese who had not known the horrors of the Great Leap Forward and the kind of devastation that could be wrought by fake propaganda.

Once the air of panic had set in, Mao launched what came to be known as the Cultural Revolution—a complete destruction of all types of autonomous thinking, comprising of universities, traditional art and craft as well as any form of religious expression. Massive armies of Red Guards were ordered to shut down colleges and universities. Members of the intelligentsia, artists and professionals from cities were deported to the countryside, supposedly to be 're-educated' through hard manual work, but were actually put into forced labour on fields and in mines. As the waves of chaos in society reached a fever pitch, Mao imposed martial law in September 1967 ostensibly to maintain law and order, but, in effect, bringing himself back as the unchallenged power centre of the country.

Once he had assumed complete control of the domestic politics, Mao began setting himself up as a major player on the international stage as well. To this end he met the president of the US, Richard Nixon, in 1972—an event that announced to the world the emergence of a new power centre in world politics.

Four years later, on 18 September 1976, the 82-year-old Mao died from complications arising out of Parkinson's disease.

Legacy

On his death, Mao left behind a two-sided legacy in China. On one hand were the rampant human rights violations, the destruction of traditional arts and Chinese culture as well as a clampdown on democratic opinion for all time to come, while on the other was the emergence of China from an overpopulated, weak, agricultural nation to a self-reliant, industrial and economic powerhouse that eventually turned out to be the biggest Asian financial success story.

Despite all the criticism about his methods, Mao continues to be regarded as a towering figure in the history of revolutions in the modern world. He spearheaded the biggest social, political and economic changes in the most populous country in the world, thus impacting the largest number of lives on the planet.

Fascinating Facts

- In all his years of ruling China, Mao rarely went near an office—instead, he passed orders from within his sprawling house, often from his bedroom.
- As part of the Great Leap Forward, Mao ordered the Great Sparrow Campaign, which entailed the destruction of sparrows because they supposedly ate all the grains. The killing of sparrows had the exact opposite effect, allowing crop-eating insects to multiply, thus leading to poor harvests.
- According to a memoir titled *The Private Life of Chairman Mao* by one of his doctors, Li Zhisui, Mao, at the peak of his power, led a dissolute life in private—overeating, chain-smoking and virtually maintaining a harem of young girls.

10. Ho Chi Minh

The short wiry man smiled when he heard the nickname 'Uncle Ho'. But behind the amiable expression was a steely determination that would later sharpen into ruthless despotism. This was Ho Chi Minh—a Vietnamese revolutionary who would ring the death knell of French colonialism in this tiny Southeast Asian country. He would not only go on to establish the Democratic Republic of Vietnam in North Vietnam but also engage their anti-communist southern neighbour, despite the latter being backed by the more powerful United States of America.

Early Life

The Vietnamese leader was born as Nguyễn Sinh Cung on 19 May 1890 and grew up in a small Central Vietnamese village, Hoằng Trú, which was then part of French Indochina. His father Nguyễn Sinh Sắc was an aspiring bureaucrat who spent long years preparing for the Confucian civil service exams. During this time, young Nguyễn and his siblings were mainly brought up by their mother Hoàng Thị Loan who, despite working at the family paddy field, would entertain the children with stories about Vietnamese folk heroes and legendary characters. It is likely that such an upbringing filled young Nguyễn with pride for his Vietnamese identity which later inspired him with a nationalistic fervour.

Nguyễn Sr worked for a while as a schoolteacher in the village. There were many times when lessons meant for much older students were easily learnt by his son. Not surprisingly, when young Nguyễn was ten years old, his father gave him another name, Nguyễn Tất Thành, meaning 'Nguyễn the Accomplished'. He would eventually take the name Ho Chi Minh, which means 'Bringer of Light.'

Soon, the family moved to Hue where young Ho started attending school and became acquainted with Confucian philosophy and Chinese literature. In 1901, Ho experienced one of the saddest events of his childhood — the death of his mother. Eventually, he enrolled in a French school and graduated with a professional degree.

Despite getting a secure job as a government school teacher, Ho was troubled by a feeling of discontent. He yearned to see more of the world, and to this end, in 1911, he gave up his job to become a cook's assistant on a ship that was to sail from Asia to Africa and Europe. The long sea voyage introduced Ho to different civilizations and cultures. The more he encountered various races and systems of government, the more he was convinced of the exploitative intention at the heart of all colonial policies. Even in the US, where he witnessed the value of freedom in the American way of life, Ho could recognize covert racial discrimination which ultimately privileged the white population over Americans of African and Asian origin.

Political Beginnings

During that time the world was plunged into the horrors of World War I. While the colonial powers like Britain, France, Italy and Spain depended on their colonies for war resources, when the time came at the end of the war to grant the subjects their right of self-determination, most baulked. Ho, too, demanded independence for Vietnam from French colonial authorities but remained unheard. Eventually, he found validation of his demands in the writings of Karl Marx who had already described imperialism as the last stage of capitalism. Ho thus found Marxism and communism more in sync with understanding the exploitation of colonized people. He decided to follow these ideologies, and in 1923, he set off for the USSR to look for allies in his fight to free Vietnam of French influence.

In USSR, Ho joined the Comintern or the Communist International and started learning all about organizing revolutions. In Moscow, especially, he found mentors who taught him how to plan and lead insurrections against even larger and better-equipped government armies. But with Soviet politics increasingly getting drawn into the conflict between Trotsky and Stalin, Ho realized that he could not expect any more help from the Soviet. So, he decided to travel to China where the political landscape was even murkier, with multiple power centres. While the Chinese hinterland was run over by local warlords, the eastern coast was the hub of rising communist influence, led by Yat-sen. General Chiang Kai-shek was another nationalist leader but was an arch-rival of the CCP.

Ho arrived in China in 1924 and was immediately sucked into the political vortex. He not only trained the local Chinese on the techniques of organizing armed struggle but also began disseminating the fundamental principles of communism among the people. In fact, he personally led an uprising of the peasants of Guangdong Province during this time. But in April 1927, Kai-shek ordered a harsh crackdown on the communists as a part of which his Kuomintang Party unleashed a wave of terror that would end with an estimated death of 3,00,000 people, including communists, supporters and even innocent villagers without affiliation to any party.

To escape the purge, Ho initially fled to Hong Kong

under an assumed name, Ly Thuy, and on a forged visa. But he was soon discovered and had to return to the USSR. From the Pacific Coast city of Vladivostok, Ho started planning his revolution and realized that he would have to set base closer to Vietnam if he were to fight the French forces occupying his homeland. To raise arms and money for his revolution, Ho, over the next thirteen years, visited many countries across Asia and Europe like Italy, India, China, the USSR and British Hong Kong.

With the outbreak of World War II, the wheel of fortune turned once again. Countries like France, which had established colonies across the world, now found themselves being threatened by their own neighbour, Germany. With France caught up in Europe, Ho thought this was the right time to launch the struggle for Vietnam's independence. In 1941, he returned to his home country with his closest supporters, Phạm Văn Đồng and Võ Nguyễn Giáp, to establish the Việt Minh, or League for the Independence of Vietnam. However, the vagaries of regional politics left their impression, and, for eighteen months, Ho was imprisoned in Kuomintang-ruled China on charges of taking part in communist activities. Back home, with growing Japanese aggression in Southeast Asia, Vietnam was again under foreign occupation.

Bid for Freedom

The end of World War II saw the exit of Japanese forces from Vietnam, and officially, at least, it was finally free. But the erstwhile French rulers were not ready to give up so easily — the French-educated emperor Bai Dao was installed by the colonial government as a puppet monarch so as to continue French influence over Vietnam's policies. Ho, by now, was determined to make a push for full Vietnamese independence. He ordered the Viet Minh forces to take as much control of the country as possible, and led by Võ Nguyễn Giáp, they were successful in seizing the northern city of Hanoi. The area under communist influence — North Vietnam — was thus declared the Democratic Republic of Vietnam, and Ho became its president.

Though based in Saigon, Emperor Bai Dao realized the inevitability of a bigger conflict, and decided to abdicate. Now known as South Vietnam, the southern part of the country, along with its capital, Saigon, was taken over by French military troops. In this way, the country ended up being divided along regional and ideological lines.

First Indochina War

As the saying goes, there are no permanent enemies or friends in politics. No sooner had Ho established his authority in North Vietnam than his old nemesis

Kai-shek began knocking on Vietnam's northern border with China. Ho was now compelled to seek the help of the same French colonial forces whom he had recently evicted from North Vietnam. But a long history of exploitation and mutual suspicion between the colonizer and the colonized made it impossible for peace to hold. In October 1946, the Vietnamese people clashed with French authorities over custom duties in the port city of Haiphong. But what followed actually triggered the First Indochina War, known as the First Indochina War. The French retaliated with a naval bombardment, which, in a span of a single afternoon, left more than six thousand Vietnamese civilians dead. Despite initial efforts by Ho to find a peaceful solution, neither side was willing to stand down, and war finally broke out in December 1946.

Fuelled by superior weaponry and wider resources, the French forces advanced to North Vietnam, even seizing Hanoi. Ho and his comrades were now compelled to escape to the countryside from where he carried on a guerrilla struggle against the French. He chose hit-and-run tactics as well as his superior knowledge of the terrain to mount attacks on the larger and better-equipped French army.

Fortunately for Ho, some foreign aid was also forthcoming. One of his supporters was now China, where the determined communist Mao Zedong had replaced Kai-shek as its most powerful leader. Communist-ruled USSR, too, offered the support of arms and resources to the Viet Minh. The results of such aid bore fruit, and in the Battle of Dien Bien Phu, the French army suffered a resounding defeat. Bled by Ho's guerrilla warfare, the French forces finally agreed to pull out completely from Vietnam. Dismayed by the huge loss of lives on both sides—a staggering 3,00,000 Vietnamese civilians were dead while the French casualties amounted to 90,000—the Geneva Convention stepped in. It made Ho the de facto president of North Vietnam and placed Ngô Đình Diệm, a pro-US leader, in charge of South Vietnam. The most significant decision of the Convention, however, was the calling of general elections across Vietnam in 1956.

The Vietnam War

With the entry of the US in Indochina politics, things took a more strident turn. Based on its theory of domino effect, the US feared that the victory of communism in one country—like in China—would influence other countries to follow similar ideological lines, and eventually communism would emerge as the dominant political system in Southeast Asia—an anathema to a hardcore capitalist country like the US. Thus, it ordered Ngô Đình Diệm to cancel the elections of 1956—an action which aroused the ire of Ho and the Việt Cộng government which was seeking to extend its control over the entire country and unify it in the process.

Once again, the northern and southern halves of Vietnam were locked in a struggle. Each was supported by its respective allies— Ho in the north by communist China and USSR, while capitalist nations like the US, South Korea and Australia backed Ngô Đình Diệm in the south. As the Vietnam War dragged on, both sides suffered heavy losses in terms of men and resources. The worst affected were the common people who were forced to bear the brunt of not only military conflict but also famine, disease and the destruction of their livelihood. Ho saw all this and decided to launch a massive offensive to force the war to its conclusion. Known as the Tet Offensive, it was planned as an all-out simultaneous attack on all major cities in Vietnam. Though taken aback initially, the southern forces and its American allies quickly rallied and launched devastating counter-attacks on the Việt Cộng forces.

The Tet Offensive failed in its immediate aim of defeating the South Vietnamese forces. However, it resulted in the world community decrying the long-drawn-out war in Vietnam and the mounting humanitarian crisis. Added to this was America's own internal opposition to the extent that, by the summer of 1967, less than 50 per cent of polled citizens supported President Johnson's conduct of the war. Calls for American pull-out both from within and without became louder.

At the opposite end of the world, Ho realized that it was just a matter of time before the US would be forced to withdraw from Vietnam, and that all he needed to do was wait. Though Ho would eventually prove to be right, he would not live to see the exit of American troops from his homeland. On 2 September 1969, Vietnam's most popular revolutionary leader suffered a heart failure and died in Hanoi—he was seventy-nine.

Legacy

In 1976, Saigon, the erstwhile capital of South Vietnam and its capitalist government, would be officially renamed Ho Chi Minh City. However, Ho's legacy extends far beyond titular changes. Brother Ho—as he was affectionately called—is remembered today in Vietnam and across the world as the chief architect of the country's independence from foreign occupation. His long struggle not only helped in freeing Vietnam from French colonial rule but later from American military influence as well. In fact, Ho's victory in the Battle of Dien Bien Phu would eventually serve as the inspiration for Algerian struggle against French colonial rule. Though in recent years, Ho's legacy has come under shadow because of the misrule of the communist government in Vietnam, he continues to stand tall as the greatest Vietnamese leader of modern times.

20 GREATEST REVOLUTIONARIES

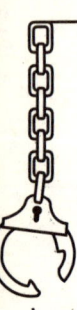

Fascinating Facts

▶ For some time, Ho worked as a waiter in Italy after his release by British authorities from Hong Kong.
▶ Vietnam is the world's largest exporter of cashew nuts, accounting for 37 per cent of the global production.

11. *Subhas Chandra Bose*

'To Delhi, To Delhi!' As this call to action rang out on a drizzly 4 July in 1944, a thrill ran down the spine of the 12,000-odd soldiers of the newly-formed Indian National Army (INA) as well as the crowd of civilians gathered at Padang, Singapore, to listen to the charismatic leader who would go down in history as the greatest Indian revolutionary of India. The man was Subhas Chandra Bose. He was the first Indian to reclaim British-ruled Indian soil when he unfurled the national flag at Port Blair's Gymkhana Ground on 30 December 1943. Today, Bose is credited not only for organizing the only strong-armed opposition to the British colonial government that ruled India for around two centuries but also for leaving a legacy of a socialist and secular vision of free India.

Early Life

Born on 23 January 1897 to a prominent Bengali family of Cuttack in Odisha, Subhas Chandra Bose grew up with the best educational opportunities. After studying at Ravenshaw Collegiate School in Cuttack, he enrolled at the prestigious Presidency College of Kolkata. However, he continued to feel restless, and abruptly took off on a tour of the well-known pilgrim sites of northern India covering Haridwar, Rishikesh, Varanasi, Mathura and Vrindavan. Eventually, he was drawn to the teachings of Ramakrishna Paramahansa and Swami Vivekananda, whose call to the Hindus of India to regain their spiritual and national courage helped Bose find his bearings.

Bose's growing nationalist fervour became apparent at this time which led him to assault an English professor at Presidency College named E.F. Oaten when the latter made disparaging remarks about India. Upon being expelled from Presidency, Bose continued his studies at Scottish Church College, from where he graduated in philosophy with first-class honours in 1919.

Bose was then packed off by his parents to England where he was supposed to study at the University of Cambridge in order to crack the Indian Civil Service examination. In 1920, he even qualified the exceedingly difficult examination, but upon hearing about the growing anti-colonial agitation in India, Bose resigned his candidacy in April 1921 and returned home.

In these years, Bose was greatly supported by his elder brother, Sarat Chandra Bose, who was an established lawyer in Calcutta as well as a member of the INC. This party had been formed in 1885 with a view to oppose British rule in India and was the main rallying point of nationalists in India at the time. Bose, too, joined the party, and under the leadership of Mahatma Gandhi, began taking part in the non-cooperation movement.

Political Beginnings

Impressed by the young man's political conviction, Gandhi advised Bose to work in Bengal under the guidance of a senior politician, Chittaranjan Das. Bose promptly proved his potential by organizing the Bengal Congress volunteers into a cohesive political force besides taking initiatives in youth education and journalism. In 1921, while Das was elected the mayor of Calcutta, Bose took charge as the chief executive officer of the Calcutta Municipal Corporation.

In 1924, Bose was arrested on charges of colluding with secret revolutionary groups operating in Bengal and was deported to Burma (present-day Myanmar). He was released in 1927 and returned to Calcutta. Thereafter, his rise in politics was rapid. Filling in the vacuum created by the demise of Das, Bose revitalized the Bengal Congress and was elected its president. Shortly afterwards, he, along with Jawaharlal Nehru, became the general secretaries of the INC. Together, the two represented the emergence of the more action-oriented and socialist section of the party as compared to Gandhi's non-violent and more pacifist approach.

Bose continued his association with underground revolutionary groups, which led to his arrest several times. While still behind bars, Bose was elected the mayor of Calcutta in 1930. Eventually, on grounds of ill health, he was released and allowed to go to Europe for treatment of tuberculosis. There, he tried to persuade the European powers to support the cause of Indian independence from British colonial rule; during this time, he also wrote *The Indian Struggle, 1920–1934*. Upon his return to India in 1936, Bose was again arrested and imprisoned for a year.

Challenge to Gandhi

With the petering out of the Civil Disobedience Movement in early 1934, Bose, like many others in the Congress Party and across India, grew increasingly certain that passive measures would never be enough to bring the colonial administration to its knees. Moreover, Bose found himself at odds with Gandhi's economic policies, which favoured agriculture and cottage industries, while Bose realized the need for India's large-scale industrialization.

Bose's popularity in the Congress Party was rising,

and in 1938, he was elected its president. One of his first measures was to form a national planning committee to give shape to his vision of widescale industrialization. This did not go down well with Gandhi, and during the elections next year, he put up a rival candidate.

Bose won again—an unequivocal assertion of his popularity in the party, and over Gandhi. However, Bose felt morally compelled to resign, believing that the public dispute with Gandhi would neither be good for the party nor for the larger struggle for Indian independence. He, instead, founded his own party called the Forward Bloc on 3 May 1939 as a way of bringing together political forces that believed in a more militant opposition to the colonial government.

Bose's initiative rattled both Indian opponents and British authorities. He was relieved from his appointment as the president of the Bengal Provincial Congress Committee and prohibited from holding any elective office for three years. The British, on the other hand, quickly moved to arrest Bose after he publicly demanded the formation of a provisional National Government in June 1940. The authorities believed that with Bose in prison, he would not be able to provide leadership to his followers, and the party would die out. In response, Bose announced his decision to go on an indefinite hunger strike, and the British authorities, scared of the repercussions, released him on condition that he would remain under house arrest.

The Great Escape

What followed has gone down in Indian history as among the most adventurous episodes related to the independence movement. One cold night in January 1941, a gentleman in the guise of a Pathan insurance agent named Mohammad Ziauddin stole out of a house on Elgin Road in Calcutta sometime past midnight. He reached Gomoh railway station and then boarded the Kalka Mail to reach Delhi. From there he reached Peshawar, and then, through the North-West Frontier, to Moscow on an Italian passport. From there, the gentleman travelled to Rome, and finally took a special courier aircraft to the German capital of Berlin. This was how Bose escaped from right under the nose of the British government in Calcutta to reach a country in Europe halfway across the world.

Being Netaji

In Germany, Bose reached out to Indian prisoners-of-war to fight for India's freedom. The result was the formation of the Indian Legion, soon rechristened Azad Hind Fauj, and then, finally, the Indian National Army. Inspired by his guidance and vision for India, his followers in Berlin honoured him with the title of Netaji or Great Leader. From here, he left for Tokyo in May 1943 where he was promised support in the form of Japanese troops and logistics.

Arrival in Singapore

Around this time, other Indians, too, had taken advantage of the British involvement in World War II to press for Indian independence. Rash Behari Bose had formed the Indian Independence League in East Asia (Singapore), and at his invitation, Netaji reached Japanese-occupied Singapore on 2 July 1943. Taking advantage of the discontent among Indian soldiers in the wake of the British retreat from Singapore—especially at their abandonment by their British officers—Netaji galvanized volunteers of the INA into a disciplined fighting force.

On 21 October the same year, at Cathay Cinema Hall in Singapore, Netaji announced the formation of the Provisional Government of Free India, and soon after, fortified by Japanese troops, he declared war on Britain. Over the next year, Netaji travelled intensively through Southeast Asia, recruiting more soldiers and lobbying for help in the form of funds and resources in his fight against the British colonial government. At the same time, he appealed to the 'home front' to keep up their support for the INA and to have faith in his efforts to free India.

Journey Back into India

On 14 April 1944, Netaji decided to attack the British by leading the INA from the eastern front. He crossed the

Burmese border and reached Moirang in Manipur where he planted the Indian national tricolour flag—a highly symbolic gesture reclaiming Indian soil from foreign occupation. However, dogged by bad weather and delay in Japanese reinforcements, he was unable to take Kohima and Imphal. The INA had to retreat to Burma, and after a brief stop at Bangkok, Bose reached Singapore on 24 April 1944.

Mystery Around His Death

With Japanese Emperor Hirohito announcing the country's surrender on 15 August 1945, Bose realized that he would have to leave Southeast Asia. However, the plane in which he was travelling on 18 August crashed around Taipei, and he reportedly died in a Japanese hospital in Taiwan as a result of burn injuries. He was supposedly cremated, and his ashes were placed at the Renkō-ji temple in Tokyo.

Such has been Netaji's charisma that, for several decades, his supporters in India and abroad refused to believe in the official account of his death. In India, there have been three commissions of inquiry till date tasked to solve the mystery behind Netaji's death. While the first two commissions concluded that he had died in the plane crash, the third, led by retired Justice M.K. Mukherjee, claimed that there was no documentary proof of such a plane crash over Taipei at that date and that the ashes at

Renkō-ji temple were not his. However, the findings of the Mukherjee Commission were rejected by the Indian government.

Legacy

Though the INA was unable to defeat the British forces, Bose's initiative sounded a warning call to the colonial government. Many historians have pointed out that more than Gandhi's non-violent movements, it was actually the threat posed by the INA that made the British leave India. They realized that after INA, they could not take the loyalty of its soldiers in the British Indian army and navy for granted, and keeping in mind its weakened situation post-World War II, thought it more prudent to withdraw from India.

Netaji's legacy has been complicated because of him receiving support from the Axis forces during World War II. However, based on his own writings, it is clear that the decision to engage Axis help was based on pragmatic considerations, and never to support fascist and Nazi excesses.

The party established by Netaji exists till this day in Bengal as the All India Forward Bloc. But more than through this party, Netaji's vision of a socialist and industrialized India was realized in the drafting of its constitution as well as government policies after independence.

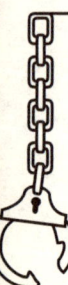

Fascinating Facts

▶ Netaji's soul-stirring slogan 'You give me blood, I promise you freedom' was delivered at a speech in Burma on 4 July 1944.

▶ Such is the regard for Netaji in Japan that on 23 August 2007, Japanese prime minister Shinzō Abe visited the Subhas Chandra Bose memorial hall in Calcutta to pay his respects to the great leader of the Indian independence movement.

▶ It was while writing about his Indian Struggle during his convalescence in Austria that Bose fell in love with his pretty typist Emilie Schenkl. The two got married in 1937 and they had a daughter, Anita Bose Pfaff.

12. Michael Collins

As the sky brightened, the last few tendrils of mist disappeared—sunny mornings in Woodfield never failed to amaze this tall, handsome man, though he had grown up in the midst of these rolling hills. But today, he was smiling at another thought as well—10,000 pound sterling—not bad, though it could be better. After months of wreaking havoc on the British security network and eluding capture, this was the price that the British government had put on the head of Michael Collins—Ireland's most dynamic and resourceful revolutionary leader. It was mainly because of his diplomatic and military skills that most of Ireland was freed from direct British rule and the Irish Free State founded in December 1921.

Early Life

Born on 16 October 1890 near Clonakilty in the Irish county of West Cork, Michael Collins grew up on the family farm named Woodfield. His father was a successful farmer and a proud Irishman who had once been part of the republican Fenian movement. But he had left all that to settle down to a life of farming, and marriage with a woman thirty-seven years younger to him. Young Collins was the youngest of eight children, and by the time he turned six, his father had passed away.

However, Collins had a comfortable childhood at home. He was educated at the local primary school and then at the Lisavair National School. There he was greatly inspired by a teacher named Denis Lyons who was a member of a nationalist secret organization named the Irish Republican Brotherhood (IRB). Young Collins was also influenced by tales of Irish history, culture and heroism in the face of British oppression.

When aged just fifteen, young Collins decided to make his way in the world and left school. Having successfully taken the British Civil Service examination in Cork in February 1906, he landed the job of a postal clerk in London and moved to the bustling metropolis. Along with a full-time job, Collins continued his education in London and enrolled at King's College. Here, he met more people determined to further the Irish nationalist cause.

He started by joining a cultural society called the Gaelic League and then moved on to become a member of the IRB. In 1915, he left for a one-year stint at the Guaranty Trust Company in New York.

Growing Activism

By the time Collins returned to Ireland in 1916, he was a towering six-foot-plus handsome young man with persuasive, resourceful charm—people loved or hated him, but rarely remained indifferent to his magnetic personality.

Collins found these traits helpful in making his way through the top echelons of Irish nationalist politics. His acute planning and courageous participation in the Easter Rising of 1916 won him many supporters, and after his release from a British prison, he was warmly welcomed into the Sinn Féin—an Irish nationalist party that was determined to gain independence from Britain by any means, even violence, if necessary.

Irish War of Independence

In the 1918 general election that allowed for the election of Irish MPs to the British House of Commons in London, Collins won a seat from Cork South. However, the Sinn Féin MPs announced that instead of joining the London government, they would form their own government in Dublin. Anticipating trouble, Sinn Féin leaders like Éamon de Valera were arrested.

In this situation, Collins took on the responsibility of convening the first Irish parliament known as Dáil Éireann at the Mansion House, Dublin, in January 1919. The Dáil officially announced an Irish Republic as well as the formation of an executive body that would eventually govern the country. Along with his political acumen, Collins was known for his strategic skills. In April 1919, he helped de Valera escape Lincoln Prison, an event that caused as big a blow to the British administration as it was a boost to the Irish nationalist forces.

In the ensuing Irish War of Independence, Collins grew both in power and reputation. He now headed the Irish nationalist intelligence network and was responsible for destroying much of the British assets. Collins also planned devastating guerrilla attacks on British security forces—a particular highlight was the November 1920 attack in which many of Britain's leading intelligence agents in Ireland were killed. Furthermore, he was made the minister for finance, and in this role, against all realistic expectations, he was successful in issuing a large bond in the form of a 'National Loan' to fund the new Irish Republic.

Treaty

Weakened by constant depletion of their military and political resources, Britain offered truce in the summer of 1921. Collins and Griffith were nominated by de Valera to lead treaty negotiations which continued from October till December. Collins realized the necessity of ending months of armed conflict so that peace could return to Ireland. With this in mind, he agreed to the British condition of Irish allegiance to the Crown in exchange of dominion status for Ireland. Even as Collins succeeded in convincing Griffith of the practicality of the treaty, he was aware of the opposition he would face back in Ireland. The treaty was signed in December 1921 and marked the creation of the Irish Free State.

Just as Collins had expected, the treaty was met with strong opposition from other Sinn Féin leaders in Ireland. De Valera in particular was incensed that Collins had gone ahead without consulting members of the cabinet, while others believed that the cause of Irish nationalism had been sold short. Drawing upon the charisma of his personality, Collins persuaded the majority of the Dáil of the practicality of the terms of the treaty. In late June 1922, Collins even won the support of Irish people in favour of the settlement.

Civil War and Death

A small extremist faction of the Dáil remained opposed to the treaty. This group not only kept obstructing the working of the provisional government, of which Collins was now the chairman, but also began carrying out armed hostilities like occupying the Four Courts in Dublin in April 1922. Collins, who had for long been trying to work out a compromise between pro- and anti-treaty factions, was now forced to act. He ordered the bombing of the Four Courts till the insurgents surrendered — an act that led to the Irish Civil War.

Collins once again took charge of the military operations — this time against the anti-treaty faction of the IRA. Under Collins, the Irish Free State forces were not only in charge of Dublin but also took control of Muster and the west which had been the anti-treaty insurgents' stronghold. As part of these operations that went on from July to August 1922, Collins returned to his home county, Cork, much against the advice of his security officers. There, on 22 August 1922, while returning from Bandon to Cork city, Collins' convoy was ambushed — he was the only casualty in the ensuing gun battle that lasted for twenty minutes.

Legacy

According to reports from the time, around 5,00,000 mourners attended Collins' funeral in Dublin — approximately one-fifth of the then Irish population. This was just one of the many testimonies to the immense popularity that Collins enjoyed across free Ireland. His sharp intelligence and strategic instinct had not only succeeding in crippling the British intelligence network in Ireland but his personal charisma and diplomatic skills had more than once gained favour for difficult political propositions. Indeed, de Valera was reported to have commented in 1966 on the legacy of Collins, 'It is my considered opinion that in the fullness of time, history will record the greatness of Collins and it will be recorded at my expense.' Above all, Collins' vision for Ireland was dignity with peace and stability, and for this he realized that he may have to pay with his life. Eventually, the Irish Civil War ended with the formation of the first free government in Ireland.

Fascinating Facts

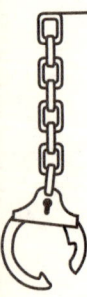

- Collins, because of his towering height, was nicknamed 'The Big Fellow' by the British intelligence forces.
- The Irish language is called Gaelic in which Sinn Féin means 'We Ourselves'.
- As a child, Collins was a very good athlete and particularly enjoyed wrestling.
- At the time of his death, Collins was engaged to a vivacious Irish woman named Catherine 'Kitty' Kiernan. The couple's plans for a November 1922 wedding were brutally ended by Collins' murder in August 1922.

13. Birsa Munda

The October breeze blowing through the dense sal forests made a pleasant rustling sound. Even more welcome was its cool touch, which invigorated the young tired man hiding in the dark shadows. He wondered how much longer he and his increasingly smaller band of rebels could hold out against the powerful British police equipped with guns and informers. But Birsa Munda was not ready to give up yet. A revolutionary leader from the tribal lands of eastern India, he is today remembered for organizing a short but intense uprising of tribal people against the economic and social oppression carried out as official policy by the British colonial government as well as their Indian agents. Birsa was also a reformer, and encouraged his followers to preserve their folk culture.

Early Life

Birsa Munda was born on 15 November 1875 in Ulihatu, Khunti, in the present-day state of Jharkhand, India. His father, Suguna Munda, was an agricultural labourer, which is why Birsa's early childhood was marked by repeated dislocation, as the family would keep moving to find work. Even then, young Birsa managed to obtain a few years of formal schooling at Salga. The school was run by Jaipal Nag, who, noticing Birsa's intelligence, persuaded his family to send him to the German Mission School.

Here, for the first time, Birsa encountered the Christian proselytizing movement against which he was to rise later. At the German Mission School, young Birsa was converted to Christianity and given a new name, Birsa David. Even as a young boy, Birsa hated the harsh attitude of the missionaries, and after a few years at the school, he left.

Growing Activism

Birsa's family moved to a place called Chaibasa where they lived from 1886 to 1890. Here, he became more and more aware of the destruction that British economic policies had caused to the tribal people's original way of life. Birsa saw how the colonial government and the Indian middlemen were colluding to loot the natural resources of the region, like metal ores and forest land, especially in the protected Porhat area. Non-tribal people from outside were being brought to cut down forests and settle down — thus grabbing land that, for generations, had sustained the tribal way of life.

Then, there was the virtually forced conversion of the tribal people into Christianity by European missionaries that received the tacit support of the colonial government. Tribal people were brainwashed into believing that their religion and traditional practices were savage, and the only development lay in embracing Christianity. More importantly, this conversion was underlined by the lure of food and money which often compelled poverty-stricken tribal people to join the tribe.

Birsa had rejected the Christian convert's life and now began searching for another philosophy strong enough to serve as an alternative to his people. During this time he met a Vaishnava monk and was deeply influenced by his teachings, which included stories from ancient Hindu epics like the Ramayana and the Mahabharata. According to some later historical accounts, Birsa even adopted Hindu customs such as wearing the sacred thread and the white garments of the Vaishnavites, besides giving up meat and alcohol. However, critics who noted this also point out that Birsa was not so much enamoured of mainstream Hinduism, as he was looking for a practical alternative to the threat of Christian conversion of his people. What was more important to Birsa was that his fellow tribals should continue to preserve their original customs and practices while eschewing harmful ones like witchcraft. Eventually, he started his own socio-religious faith, called 'Birsait', which was a fusion of tribal and Hindu beliefs and practices.

Birsa, however, realized that the real source of his people's trouble was the highly exploitative economic policies forced upon the land by the British administration. And to this end he started organizing his followers during the early 1890s to rise up against the colonial government. The movement he launched was called the 'Ulgulan' or 'The Great Tumult'. Armed with weapons of the forest, the simple but lethal bow and arrow, Birsa and his army would repeatedly attack British officials and assets. However, in the end, the might of the colonizer's gun and money proved stronger. The British administration not only unleashed the full force of its police force upon him but also tempted the Indian middlemen to spy on the tribal movements and reveal their whereabouts.

Death and Legacy

Eventually, after more than five years of dogged resistance, on 3 March 1900, Birsa was captured by the British police from the Jamkopai forest of Chakradharpur and imprisoned at the Ranchi jail. There, on 9 June 1900, he died—of cholera, according to British prison records—but more likely was poisoned by the guards. The courageous tribal leader and revolutionary was just twenty-five at the time of his death.

Birsa's Ulgulan against the British government was later brought into the mainstream Indian independence movement. Unlike the stories of valour about Bhagat Singh and Surya Sen, Birsa's movement appeared to have been buried for long in the leafy sal forests of the red Chota Nagpur earth. Incredibly, it was Birsa's movement which actually had a more material impact than the activities of other revolutionaries. So rattled were the British by the tribal uprising led by Birsa that the government was forced to pass the Chota Nagpur Tenancy Act in 1908. The act placed significant restrictions on the transfer of land from the tribal people to non-tribals. In this way, Birsa's movement led to the recognition of the tribal people's ancestral claim on the land and wealth of the forests in which they had been living for ages.

Today, Birsa is remembered as the most important tribal revolutionary figure in the history of India, as is evident from his portrait in the parliament which keeps company with other Indian historical leaders. Myriad structures, ranging from educational institutions and sports stadiums in Jharkhand to the international airport in Ranchi, are named after him. A host of cultural activities are organized by the Jharkhand state government on his birth anniversary every year. However, the only true way to honour his memory would be to address the real problems of the tribal population of the area which, even after seventy-one years of Indian independence, remain among the most exploited and ignored communities of the country.

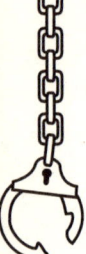

Fascinating Facts

▶ Birsa was supposed to be a skilled flute player in his childhood—he was rarely seen without his flute made of pumpkin shell.

▶ Birsa was named after the day of his birth; since he was born on Thursday, he was named Birsa, a folk adaption of the Hindi equivalent, Brihaspati.

14. Mustafa Kemal Atatürk

From the balcony of the Government House in Izmir, an undulating ocean of people is seen, fluttering the red star and crescent flags—occasionally peaking in frenzied enthusiasm. On this day in 1923, they have all turned out to catch a glimpse of their revered Pasha, Mustafa Kemal, who, having led the revolution against the foreign occupation of Turkey, has now become the founder and first president of the Turkish Republic. Equally importantly, he would be honoured as a secularist who oversaw the transformation of Turkey from a traditional society to a modern secular republic. As a mark of honour, he would be called Atatürk, meaning 'Father of the Turks'.

Early Life

Mustafa was born in 1881 in Ottoman-ruled Salonica, which is now the Greek city of Thessaloniki. His father,

Ali Rıza, used to be an official with the local militia, but later settled down into the timber business. Though Rıza died when Mustafa was just seven years old, he had already enrolled his son in a modern education system which would have a defining influence on the child's development. Interestingly, Mustafa was given the moniker of Kemal—meaning 'The Perfect One'—by his mathematics teacher as a nod to the boy's striving for perfectionism in studies. As he turned twelve, Mustafa started going to a military school, after which he moved to the military academy in Istanbul, eventually graduating as a captain from the General Staff College in 1905.

Political Turmoil

In Istanbul, Kemal was exposed to the political turmoil in the heart of Turkey. The country was then ruled by the despotic Sultan Abdul Hamid II as part of the large ailing Ottoman Empire. The local Turkish people suffered discrimination at all levels of governance, and people living off the land were especially oppressed, without modern education, healthcare and any prospect of development. All this angered Kemal who became part of secret societies to carry out anti-government activities. One of this was the Committee of Union and Progress (CUP) that had emerged from the Young Turk Movement—a revolutionary movement that vowed to bring down the authoritarian regime of the Ottoman Sultan.

Though Kemal disagreed with the popular Young Turk leader Enver Pasha on many significant aspects of the anti-government revolution, he supported the CUP when, in April 1909, it marched into Istanbul and forced the sultan to abdicate. However, Kemal being the true liberal statesman that he was, insisted on the separation of politics and the military—in the process further incurring the disapproval of Enver and other CUP members. Leading by example, Kemal distanced himself from political power and concentrated on the modernization of the Turkish armed forces. He ordered the translation of German infantry training manuals into Turkish, and enforced discipline through the command structure rather than enforcing it through personal, political and religious preferences. All these acts brought him at loggerheads with the CUP leadership, but also earned him the increasing respect of a new emerging group of young officers in the army.

Military Career

In order to distance Kemal from the nerve centre of power, the CUP decided to embroil him in military action. He thus despatched to the front lines of the tottering Ottoman Empire. First, he fought against the Italians in Libya in 1911 and then in the Balkan Wars from 1912 to 1913.

With the outbreak of World War I in 1914, after much hesitation by Enver, he was finally given command of the 19th Division, which was being organized in the Gallipoli Peninsula. Here, in 1915, Kemal led a repulsion of the Allied invasion at the Dardanelles and was hailed as the Saviour of Istanbul. Next year, he was sent to fight on the Eastern Front and became the only Turkish general (hence titled Pasha) to win any victories over the Russians. In 1917, Kemal was sent to the Ottoman provinces of Syria and Iraq which were being threatened by British invasion from Egypt. But, horrified by the poor state of the army, he resigned his commission and returned to Istanbul. For a brief while, Kemal withdrew from active duty to recuperate from a series of health problems. But, with a new sultan—Mehmed V—assuming the throne, he was sent back to Syria. There, Kemal—despite being crippled by impoverished and ill-equipped troops—tried to hold ground as best as he could till the Armistice of Mudros halted the fighting.

The Nationalist Revolution

Back in Istanbul, the CUP leaders recognized the imminent defeat of the Central Powers in World War I. Since they had sided with this alliance, they escaped to Germany, leaving Turkey at the mercy of a weak sultan and fast-approaching Allied forces. The latter imposed harsh conditions on Turkey in the guise of a peace treaty which angered Kemal. He vowed to resist the treaty, and to that end, began organizing a nationalist revolution from Anatolia in May 1919. In the meantime, Kemal also successfully repulsed Greek attempts to capture Smyrna and its hinterland. The resulting military success not only reiterated his strategic skills but also his leadership of and vision for a new nationalist Turkey.

From this new position of power, Kemal was able to renegotiate terms with the Allied powers in the Treaty of Lausanne. He now decided to take firm control of the domestic affairs in Turkey. In 1921, Kemal put in place a provisional government in Ankara which would be the new capital of a new modern Turkey. The Ottoman Sultanate was officially abolished the following year. Finally, in 1923, Turkey was declared a secular republic, with Kemal as its first president.

Modernization of Turkey

What made Kemal a true revolutionary leader was not just his emancipation of Turkey from foreign influence, but transforming it from a medieval theocratic caliphate (a state ruled by an Islamic leader known as a caliph) to a modern secular republic. To do this, he founded the Republican People's Party on 9 August 1923. This party adopted the six-pronged programme of reform, known as the 'Six Arrows'. These were republicanism, nationalism, populism, secularism, statism and revolution.

The most obvious result of this reform movement was the separation of state and religion. Religious courts were abolished and religious schools shut down. In place of the earlier Islamic law code, Kemal ordered the adoption of a new secular law code from June 1926 which was actually an amalgamation of the Swiss civil code, the Italian penal code and the German commercial code. The religious brotherhoods which had long functioned as bastions of conservatism were declared illegal.

Yet another site of Kemal's reformist plans was the educational system. In place of earlier religious schools, he ordered new secular schools which would teach Turkish in Latin rather than the Arabic script. Officially introduced in all spheres of Turkish life in November 1928, this was a change with far-reaching implications, as the youth now had access to latest western developments in science, technology and the humanities. Most importantly, primary education was made free and compulsory to all — both boys and girls. All these measures paved the way for a new secular, humanist and scientific-minded generation that boasted of one of the highest literacy rates in the Middle East.

Even more spectacular was the social change that Kemal's reforms ushered. Opening up education, voting rights and work opportunities to women meant a quantum leap in their social, political and economic states. In December 1934, women not only got the right to vote in parliamentary elections but could also contest for the seats themselves. The new law code had abolished polygamy and turned marriage into a civil contract which, in turn, eased divorce proceedings for men and women.

Among other initiatives based on the western model were adoption of the western-style headdress in 1925 to replace the traditional fez, as well as the practice of taking a surname in 1935. It was at this time that Kemal formally took on the title of Atatürk, which meant 'Father of the Turks'.

In the economic sphere, Atatürk emphasized self-reliance, and set Turkey on the path of large-scale industrialization, owned and operated by the state. This self-reliance was reflected in Atatürk's foreign policy also. He was determined that Turkey should follow a neutral path and avoid an alliance with any international bloc. At the same time, he ironed out conflicts with Greece, Iraq and Britain that had lingered in the wake of World War I.

Such an expansive, ambitious and thorough programme of reform naturally could not go unchallenged. Conservative Islamic leaders resisted erosion of age-old power structures just as minority groups like the Kurds tried to reject the strong centralized governance. Then there were individuals jealous of Atatürk's power, as a result of which he was the target of assassination attempts. To any challenge of his personal and political vision, he responded swiftly and decisively—putting down insurrections and political opposition with speed and force. The single party rule that he started continued almost without interruption until 1945.

Death and Legacy

Since his days of military campaign, Atatürk had struggled with medical issues, and from the mid-1930s, his health steadily declined. On the morning of 10 November 1938, Atatürk died of complications arising out of cirrhosis of the liver. In 1953, his body was eventually interred in a grand mausoleum built in the chosen capital of the country, Ankara.

Atatürk almost single-handedly ushered in the modern transformation of Turkey. From a medieval society ruled by a despotic sultan as part of a fast-unravelling Ottoman Empire, it turned into a modern, secular republic within a span of barely two decades. Though critics later denounced his strong centralized administration and harsh measures to crush rebellions, it is a fact that a steely hand was required to guide Turkey into the new age.

Fascinating Facts

- To popularize the use of the Latin script to write in the Turkish language, Atatürk himself toured the Turkish countryside to illustrate, with chalk in hand, the new alphabet and pronunciation system to the people.
- The changes brought about in the marriage laws appeared to be reflected in Atatürk's personal life as well—he himself got married to a woman with western education, named Latife Hanım, in 1923, though they were divorced two years later.
- According to an anecdote from the 1920s, Atatürk's introduction of western headgear set about a rush in the tailoring of hats in Istanbul, so much so that cloth turned scarce.
- One of Atatürk's adopted daughters, Sabiha Gökçen, went on to become the first female combat pilot of the world.
- Because of its weak inefficient governance, the Ottoman Empire was once upon a time known as the 'Sick Man of Europe'.

15. Josip Broz Tito

The imposing throne-like chair seems the perfect seat for the man who possessed complete power in Yugoslavia, thought the American journalist, Helen Fisher, as she waited for an answer from her subject. General Tito thoughtfully smoked his pipe and then answered in an unwavering voice that denoted confidence as much as supreme authority. After all, he was the man behind the transition of Yugoslavia from a straggling monarchy to a modern socialist federation of states. Revered as Marshal Tito, he ruled Yugoslavia in various positions for around four decades. Equally significantly, he gained international respect by refusing to be aligned to either the western capitalist or the eastern communist bloc that had come to divide the world during the Cold War. In this role, he was the founder of the Non-Aligned Movement that eventually included countries like India and Egypt.

Early Life

Broz was born into a peasant family on 7 May 1892 in Kumrovec, in the northern Croatian region of the then Austro-Hungarian Empire. Two years after completing school at Kumrovec in 1905, he left for Sisak where he was apprenticed to a machinist. Living and working in a city, he became aware of pressing political concerns of those times, like poor working conditions of industrial workers as well as rapacious capitalists. To make a difference, Broz first signed up with the union of metallurgy workers, and then, in 1910, officially joined the Social Democratic Party of Croatia and Slavonia.

World War I

With the clouds of World War I gathering over Europe, Broz enlisted in the Austro-Hungarian Army in 1913 and even went through a training course for non-commissioned officers. Despite initial foray into anti-war propaganda, Broz distinguished himself on the Eastern Front in Galicia against the Russians and was promoted to the rank of sergeant major, becoming the youngest to hold the rank in the Austro-Hungarian Army at the time. However, at the Battle of Bukovina, he was wounded and captured by the Russians.

As a prisoner-of-war in Russia, Broz got to know the

Bolsheviks and was attracted to their ideology which promised a classless society. He even took part in the October Revolution, married a Russian woman, Pelagija Belousova, and in 1918, signed up the Yugoslav section of the Russian Communist Party. With the end of the war, Broz returned to Croatia with his family and once again dove into political action. He became the formal member of the Communist Party of Yugoslavia (CPY) which put him at odds with the Yugoslavian government and even led to his imprisonment, on charges of stocking bombs at his house.

Rise to Power

After his release in March 1934, Broz took on the name of Tito. Negotiating his way through the political tumult of the times, he was careful to remain on the right side of the powerful communist leaders in the USSR. In 1937, his efforts paid off, and Tito was given the Central Committee of CPY. But before he could usher in any political changes in Yugoslavia, World War II broke out in Europe in 1939. This time Tito was determined not to let his country be forced to fight for any foreign power. To this end, he rallied his supporters to form the Partisans, who eventually became famous for offering the most effective resistance to the Axis powers in Europe.

Tito's leadership of Yugoslavia during World War II

proved beyond doubt that he was the real power centre. Any attempts by the exiled Yugoslavian royal family to return, towards the end of the war, were crushed, and in 1944, Tito declared the CPY as the ruling party of the country. With it, he became the unchallenged leader of Yugoslavia.

However, Tito was too much of a politician not to realize that until his own position was absolutely secure, he could not hope to bring any reform in the country. Thus, from 1945, began the purge during which any opposition to communism in the country, and especially to his leadership in the CPY, was brutally crushed. Even his call for general elections was an eyewash, since it was entirely rigged in his favour. His control over the party, government and country thus complete, Tito renamed his homeland as the Socialist Federal Republic of Yugoslavia.

Reforms

While widespread political and civil repression tainted Tito's rise to power, once beyond challenge, he embarked upon a programme of reforms. From the mid-1960s, private enterprise was encouraged in the economy. Many of the previously imposed restrictions on free speech and religious expression were loosened as well. On 1 January 1967, Tito made Yugoslavia the first communist country to do away with visa requirements. This opening up of its borders to all foreign visitors was indeed unthinkable at the height of the Cold War.

After Tito was elected president of Yugoslavia by the Federal Assembly for the sixth consecutive time in 1971, he brought in even more extensive political and administrative reforms. As many as twenty constitutional amendments were made, which granted wider autonomy to the provinces within Yugoslavia, and paved the way for greater decentralization of governance. Apart from crucial matters like defence, finance and foreign affairs, the provinces and republics were allowed to frame their own laws in areas like education, health and housing as long as they ensured free trade and movement within the whole of Yugoslavia. In 1974, a new constitution under Tito even equalized the smaller federal units with the two largest, Serbia and Croatia.

A World Leader

Apart from guiding his own country into the modern era, Tito also launched a new initiative on the international stage with the Non-Aligned Movement. At a time when most of the world was divided between the western and eastern camps based on the capitalist and communist systems respectively, Tito called upon like-minded nation states to take an independent line. Countries like India, Egypt, Indonesia and Ghana came together with

Yugoslavia to hold the first meeting of the non-aligned states in Belgrade in 1961. On 1 September the same year, Tito became the first secretary general of the Non-Aligned Movement, thus proving his stature as a world leader and enhancing his country's position on the global stage.

Death and Legacy

From the mid-1970s, Tito moved away from the public gaze. The personality cult that he had assiduously built continued to ensure his popularity while allowing him to shrug off the responsibilities of daily governance, like the student riots of the late 1960s. Towards the end of 1979, he became unwell and had to be hospitalized in January 1980 for an array of medical issues. On 4 May 1980, just three days before his 88th birthday, he breathed his last. He remained the unchallenged leader of Yugoslavia till the very end.

Marshal Tito, as he came to be regarded, was one of the few revolutionaries and the rare dictator whose legacy has been more positive than negative. Though it is undeniable that he used brute force to crush down political opposition in the early days, he also ushered in wide-ranging reforms in Yugoslavia. However, the decentralization would require a delicate handling of checks and balances among all the provinces—something that proved too difficult for his successors. Finally, Tito was a consummate global leader who, despite flirting with Soviet and American support at various phases, eventually charted a new non-aligned path, and even got other countries to follow suit.

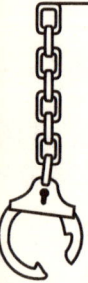

Fascinating Facts

▶ Bored with persistent poor refereeing in a football match, Tito is believed to have once barged onto the field, blown the whistle and shouted, 'Now let's see whether some oppose the decisions of the referee?'

▶ In 1972, Yugoslavia, under Marshal Tito, was the first communist country that Queen Elizabeth II decided to visit.

▶ Goli Otok, a barren island on the Adriatic/Croatian coast, was ordered to be used as a prison camp by Tito.

16. Nelson Mandela

The cold damp walls around him were like a wet rag on his spirit. 'How many more days of this crushing punishment?' the frail man wondered. But as scenes of thousands of his country people marching and singing of freedom passed through his mind's eye, the prisoner looked up again—the patch of light visible from his solitary confinement cell shone a shade brighter—and once again took up his pen. This was Nelson Mandela, South African anti-apartheid leader, Nobel Peace Prize winner and the first African-origin president of the country.

Early Life

Born as Rolihlahla Mandela on 18 July 1918 into the Madiba clan in the village of Mvezo, the future leader grew up listening to stories of African valour and ancestral heroes.

Mandela's father was the chief advisor to Jongintaba Dalindyebo, the regent of the Thembu people. When he was just twelve years old, Mandela lost his father, after which he became a ward of the royal court.

Though young Mandela got enough opportunities to study — even enrolling at the University of Fort Hare — his heart was actually in activism. Soon enough, he realized that in order to struggle for the rights of his people, the study of law would be more helpful, and with that purpose in mind, he started studying for an LLB degree from the University of the Witwatersrand.

Politics, however, turned out to be a stronger pull, and in 1944, he joined the African National Congress (ANC) which was founded to fight for the rights of the black people in South Africa. Because of its colonization by England, the country had carried on with an official policy of racial discrimination and segregation, known as apartheid, which means separateness in Afrikaans. This had resulted in extremely oppressive conditions for its non-white African majority, who were barred from the most important social, political and economic rights.

Growing Activism

In 1952, the government, made up of a predominantly white National Party, put the pass laws in place, which made it compulsory for non-white people to move around with a specific documentation, especially in areas reserved for white people. Mandela initiated a non-violent struggle against this law, because of which he travelled across the country. His activism at this time culminated in the Freedom Charter in 1955, for which like-minded African leaders came together to draft a document that demanded non-racial social democracy in South Africa.

The government responded with harsh treason laws and arrested anti-apartheid activists, including Mandela. Among the most brutal instances of government repression was the 1960 massacre of unarmed black South Africans by the police at Sharpeville. In 1961, after his release from prison, Mandela felt compelled to change strategies and decided to meet state violence with guerrilla tactics. He was captured in 1962, and in the trial held next year — infamous as the Rivonia trial — was sentenced to life imprisonment.

Period Behind Bars

For the next eighteen years, Mandela was incarcerated at the Robben Island prison off Cape Town, then transported to Pollsmoor Prison and finally to Victor Verster Prison near Paarl. During his 26-year-long period of incarceration, Mandela received several offers of release from the government if he would agree to give up his political activism. Finally, with no sign of Mandela losing domestic support, and with the international community's condemnation of the imprisonment rising, the new South African government under President F.W. de Klerk agreed to the unconditional release of Mandela. This was followed by his assuming the leadership of the ANC. Eventually he was successful in negotiating with de Klerk for a peaceful transition to non-racial democracy in South Africa.

Presidency

Not surprisingly, the ANC swept South Africa's first elections by universal suffrage in April 1994. Mandela was sworn in as the president of the first multi-racial government of the country. As part of his plans to improve the social and economic conditions of the black people, he introduced various developmental policies like housing, education, jobs and economic opportunities. Another significant initiative was the Truth and Reconciliation Committee set up in 1995 to investigate and order reparation of atrocities committed on the black population during the apartheid years. As president, Mandela also supervised the drawing up of a new democratic constitution of South Africa which came into effect in 1996.

Despite his overwhelming popularity, Mandela declined a second presidential term and made way for his close aide and ANC presidential successor, Thabo Mbeki. Mandela instead diverted all his energy and time into the Nelson Mandela Foundation established in 1999 to streamline his work for peace and social justice. With other senior, well-regarded world leaders, Mandela also founded The Elders, an international group working towards community service and conflict resolution not just in South Africa but across the world. On his ninetieth birthday, the venerable South African leader was feted by numerous countries, and in 2009, the UN announced that henceforth his birthday—18 July—would be celebrated each year as Nelson Mandela International Day.

On 5 December 2013, Mandela succumbed to a chronic respiratory tract infection at his home in Johannesburg; he was ninety-five.

Legacy

Mandela has been the most revered public figure of South Africa. He will always be remembered for his determined struggle, from behind the bars, to end apartheid and his sincerity in improving the lives of fellow Africans through countless government policies. But, more importantly, he showed the way ahead for multi-racial living through peace and mutual understanding. His autobiography, *Long Walk to Freedom*, encapsulates his illustrious life. Former state president, de Klerk, after Mandela's death, described him as a 'unifier' and as one who, despite his sufferings, stood out for 'a remarkable lack of bitterness'—all signs of not only a great revolutionary leader but of 'a man', as then US president Barack Obama said, 'who took history in his hands and bent the arc of the moral universe towards justice'.

Fascinating Facts

- Mandela was affectionately called by his clan name, Madiba.
- He was named Nelson by his teacher Ms Mdingane at the primary school in Qunu, according to the prevalent practice of giving Christian names to students.
- Mandela's support was a key factor in helping South Africa win the bid to host the 2004 FIFA World Cup.
- In 1990, Mandela was awarded the Bharat Ratna, and in the year 1992, Pakistan bestowed upon him the Nishan-e-Pakistan.

17. Che Guevara

A pair of intense questioning eyes gazing at a not-so-distant horizon, wispy hair escaping from a revolutionary-insignia-marked beret and a look of quiet determination set in a black-and-white photo clicked by Cuban photographer Alberto Korda on 5 March 1960 has now become an icon of any anti-establishment statement. The person behind the image is Che Guevara, Argentine-born revolutionary who played an integral role in the Cuban Revolution and was among the first to develop the doctrine of guerrilla warfare, inspiring generations to be inspired by his anti-imperialist ideology.

Early Life

Born as Ernesto Guevara de la Serna on 14 June 1928 in Rosario, Argentina, the future revolutionary leader grew up in a family that held socialist views. As a child,

Guevara suffered from asthma, but that did not keep him from excelling both in studies and sports. After completing school, he enrolled at the University of Buenos Aires to study medicine.

During his college years, Guevara travelled extensively across Central and South America. Passing through villages across the continent, he was deeply affected by the poverty of the people and the exploitation of the poor at the hands of the powerful, especially the wealthy landowning class. Guevara became convinced more than ever that armed revolution was the only way to free people from the shackles of feudalism and inequality.

The Motorcycle Diaries

Of particular significance was a nine-month journey that Guevara took along with his friend Alberto Granado in December 1951, during a break from his medical studies. The two started from Argentina, passed through Chile, then Peru and Colombia till they reached Venezuela. From there Guevara alone travelled further to Miami before taking a flight to return to Argentina. Reflections on the land and its people during this journey would find their way into Guevara's journal which was later published posthumously by his family as *The Motorcycle Diaries: Notes on a Latin American Journey* in 2003, and the next year adapted into a film titled *The Motorcycle Diaries*.

Growing Activism

The travels not only convinced Guevara of the need to be politically active if changes were to be brought in society, but also led to a new awareness of a common Latin American identity. Unlike the mainstream political ideology of the time, he saw the different states in Central and South America not as separate entities, each with its own problems, but as unified by similar economic and social institutions. Increasingly, he came to believe that liberation of these people would require more than local agitations—a broader vision and a pan-continental strategy.

This realization took Guevara to Guatemala in 1953 where a revolutionary leader Jacobo Árbenz had done away with long-held feudal systems to set up a progressive, socialist government. However, just the next year, Árbenz was brought down by a US government-backed coup. The dismissal of Árbenz and the interference of the Central Intelligence Agency (CIA) convinced Guevara of deep-seated American resistance to any form of leftist political dispensation in Latin America. As a result, Guevara realized that in order to bring about lasting socio-economic revolution, American influence would have to be combated and defeated.

Cuban Connection

From Guatemala, Guevara decided to head to Mexico where he met the Castro brothers whose revolutionary forces challenged the dictatorial regime of Fulgencio Batista in Cuba. Though Guevara initially joined Fidel Castro's 26th of July movement as a doctor for the revolutionary force, the young Argentine's weapons training came handy, as the rebels were pushed back by Batista's forces to Sierra Maestra. From the safety of these hilly enclaves, Castro's men now began regrouping and employing hit-and-run tactics like ambush, raids and sabotage that would come to be known as guerrilla warfare. Eventually, this would turn out to be a deadly weapon in the hands of smaller-sized mobile rebels to bleed out larger, traditional armies.

Guevara, during this time, emerged as a complex, multi-faceted personality. He would not only fine-tune the guerrilla tactics of Castro's forces and treat wounded men but also order the execution of suspected traitors. A glimpse into this period of fighting the Batista government would be found in Guevara's memoirs titled *Pasajes De La Guerra Revolucionaria* in Spanish and published in 1963 and later translated as *Episodes of the Cuban Revolutionary War* which was published in 1968. The ruthless aspect of his personality became even more prominent when, after Castro's capture of Havana on 8 January 1959, Guevara took charge of the La Cabana prison and ordered the executions of many suspected to be opposed to the revolution.

Guevara now formally adopted Cuban citizenship and was invited to assume important roles in Castro's communist government. Guevara became the chief of the Industrial Department of the National Institute of Agrarian Reform and the president of the National Bank of Cuba. As the minister of industry, he brought about sweeping reforms like the nationalization of industry as well as redistribution of land. Guevara also travelled to many countries as the ambassador of a new communist Cuba, expounding its policies and looking for fresh international alignments. In all this, Guevara's measures, both at home and abroad, would be underlined by deep anti-American and pro-Soviet tendencies. All these measures of the early 1960s would be powerfully recorded in many of his speeches and writings, most significantly in the 1965 published *El socialismo y el hombre en Cuba* and its English translation titled *Man and Socialism in Cuba* published in 1967.

Guerrilla Theory

The other important book by Guevara was his manual of guerrilla warfare titled *La guerra de guerrillas* in Spanish and *Guerrilla Warfare* in English which was published in 1961. This outlined his doctrine of Latin American revolution based on three fundamental principles. The first was the belief in the possibility of a large traditional army being defeated by a guerrilla force. The second was the idea that for a revolution to start, it was not necessary for all the conditions to be present — in fact, a rebellion could bring into existence some of the supporting factors of a revolution. The third was Guevara's recognition that the Latin American countryside with its hills and impenetrable jungles was particularly suited for guerrilla warfare. Guevara's handbook would go on to become highly influential, and an important resource to guerrilla forces in other parts of the world as well.

Growing Disillusionment

Despite Guevara's best efforts at bringing about a more egalitarian economic system in Cuba, some of his reformist measures began to fail. His persistent opposition to the US resulted in economic sanctions on Cuba that hit its economy hard. Even worse, his hopes of Soviet assistance turned sour as he realized that the communist giant was only interested in treating Cuba as a captive market for its products. Soviet Russia's quick exit from Cuban waters during the height of the Cuban missile crisis of 1962 without consulting the Cuban leadership disillusioned him further. He made no effort to mince words at an address to the UN General Assembly in December 1964 in which he blamed the US for intrusion in Cuban airspace as well as its economic woes.

New Revolutionary Goals

Sometime after his return from New York, Guevara disappeared from public gaze and went untraceable. For at least two years no one knew about his movements and involvement. He had not only resigned from his ministerial office but had also given up his Cuban citizenship.

Eventually it turned out that Guevara had left with his band of guerrillas for what is now the Democratic Republic of the Congo. There he had intended to assist Patrice Lumumba, Congo's first freely elected prime minster, in the Congo Civil War which was made murkier by interference of bigger powers like the US, the USSR and Belgium. Over a series of armed conflicts, Guevara and his soldiers lost, while Lumumba was captured on the orders of army chief Joseph-Désiré Mobutu and executed. Guevara fled at first to Tanzania and then to a hidden location in a village near Prague.

Guevara's next revolutionary destination, Bolivia, would prove to be his last. He landed there in late 1966, his head shaved and his trademark beard gone. Thus disguised, Guevara began organizing forces to launch guerrilla attacks against the Bolivian Army in the area of Santa Cruz. Despite some initial successes, Guevara's band was quickly demolished by the Bolivian Army supported by the CIA during an especially fierce conflict on 8 October 1967. It ended with Guevara being wounded, captured and killed.

Legacy

Like the man himself, Guevara's legacy has been complex. His detractors point out that the man who trained to be a doctor was responsible for ordering executions in cold blood. On the other hand are stories about how he would continue to lead the hard life of a revolutionary even after becoming a minister. Setting a personal example to the voluntary labour programme after the Cuban Revolution, Guevara himself worked on sugarcane plantations during the rare hours away from his ministerial duties. Most importantly, Guevara realized the need for all anti-imperialist and anti-colonial forces to come together. His revolutionary missions were not limited to his own or adopted country but extended to wherever there were exploitative, capitalist regimes to be vanquished.

Over the years, Guevara's legacy has come to influence different causes and sections of humanity. While his guerrilla forces failed to win in Congo and Bolivia, his staunch anti-imperialistic stance reverberated ironically in the heart of America during the civil protests of the 1960s. Even more remarkably, his image has been appropriated by capitalist-money-fuelled popular culture and is now commonly seen on T-shirts, mugs as well as restaurant décor as markers of a hip, anti-establishment radicalism. Though in ways he may have never intended or foreseen, Guevara's legacy remains alive and kicking.

Fascinating Facts

- The bike after which Guevara titled his journal *The Motorcycle Diaries* was nicknamed 'Powerful'. Ironically, it broke down shortly after the journey began.
- After he died, Guevara's hands were cut off to preserve his fingers in formaldehyde so that his identity could be confirmed by the CIA.
- As president of the National Bank of Cuba, Guevara simply signed currency as 'Che', indicating his famed disdain for capitalist theories of economy.

18. Fidel Castro

The bullet hit the side of the refrigerator used to store life-saving medicines—announcing yet another skirmish with Batista's forces. But the man at the centre of it all was used to violence by now. Fidel Castro was determined to see the rebellion through, and eventually his grit and perseverance would pay. In 1959, Castro would set up the only communist state in the western half of the world. He would remain the absolute ruler of Cuba for five decades during which wide-ranging social, political and economic reforms would be ushered in the country. Though international observers would criticize his methods, human rights violations as well as the long-term effect of communism on Cuban economy, Castro would emerge as a force to reckon with—having brought even a mighty superpower such as the US on the verge of a nuclear showdown at the height of the Cold War.

Early Life

The Cuban leader was born as Fidel Alejandro Castro Ruz on 13 August 1926 near Birán, in Cuba's eastern Oriente Province as the illegitimate son of a sugar plantation owner, Ángel Castro. When Castro turned fifteen, his mother married Ángel, and two years later, he was formally recognized as Ángel's son. This mixed upbringing, however, did not affect young Castro's opportunities, as he was given the best education money could buy. As a child he was sent to private Jesuit boarding schools. He graduated from El Colegio de Belén in late 1945 and finally enrolled at the University of Havana to study law, where his political involvement began.

At the time, Cuba suffered from widespread economic disparity in society. While foreign industrialists and plantation owners enjoyed a lavish style of living, poor farmers and industrial labourers continued to toil in the most miserable conditions for generations without any hope of a better life. Despite growing up in material comfort himself, Castro deeply felt the injustice of the present system and gravitated towards socialism which offered the promise of a classless society. Castro's political longings even took him to Dominican Republic in 1947 where he had the intention of taking part in a coup against Dominican leader Rafael Trujillo. But the bid to depose Trujillo failed, and Castro fled back to Cuba.

Locking Horns with Batista

At home, Castro began supporting the Cuban leader Eduardo Chibás, and his party, Partido Ortodoxo. They not only demanded action to weed out deep-rooted corruption in the government but also other economic reforms and legal freedom from foreign influence, especially the American corporate houses. However, Chibás was unable to stem the rise of General Batista who led a coup in 1952 resulting in the cancelling of the general elections, and installing himself as the sole power centre in Cuba.

Castro retaliated by leading an insurrection against Batista on 26 July 1953. But the attack on the Moncada Barracks was foiled, and Castro was arrested and then sentenced to fifteen years in prison. However, this led to an outpouring of public anger from all corners of the country. Castro had come to symbolize the only voice of opposition against Batista's dictatorial regime. Reading the mood on the ground, Batista offered an amnesty deal to Castro in 1955 by which he was freed from prison.

Support from Guevara

After his release, Castro decided to seek outside support for his political action, and to this end, he left for Mexico. There he met up with Argentine-born charismatic revolutionary Che Guevara who was an ardent communist, since he believed that this was the only system that could improve the conditions of the poor. Having enlisted Guevara's help both in terms of ideology and resources, Castro eventually decided to return to Cuba.

An attack on Batista's forces was planned on 2 December 1956. To bring this about, Castro landed with eighty-one supporters on the eastern city of Manzanillo. But the conflict resulted in the rebels' defeat, and Castro was lucky to be able to escape with brother Raul and Guevara into the forests of the Sierra Maestra mountain range along the island's south-eastern coast.

Castro was, however, determined to continue with his opposition to the Batista government. In this goal, he was assisted by Guevara's superior knowledge of guerrilla warfare. Before long, the rebels were employing quick hit-and-run tactics to mount successively deadlier attacks on Batista's forces. This continued from 1956 to 1958 during which Castro had even started running a parallel government in the villages of the remote Sierra Maestra ranges.

Eventually, Castro's persistent opposition began inspiring other parts of Cuba. The general population had long been seething at the rampant corruption of the Batista government and its brutal taxation policies. Now even sections of the army began showing signs of mutiny. Castro realized that the time was right to launch an offensive. In 1958, he ordered a series of military strikes against the government forces throughout Cuba. This time the rebels had no trouble capturing major cities, and by the end of the year, it was clear that Castro's revolution was underway. In January 1959, Batista fled to the Dominican Republic, leaving Castro to take charge of the country.

Reforms

Initially, Castro installed José Miró Cardona as the prime minister of the new Cuban government while he assumed the position of the commander-in-chief of the armed forces. But upon Cardona's sudden resignation in 1959, Castro took over as the country's prime minister—thus completing his rise to the top of the political ladder.

Castro now ushered in a series of reforms in Cuba. Among the most important of such measures was the nationalization of farms and factories. The First Agrarian Reform Law of May 1959 not only limited the size of land holdings but also prohibited any property ownership by foreigners in Cuba. The reforms were intended to improve the conditions of small farmers and labourers by freeing them from the rapacious control of landlords and big industrialists. But eventually, production suffered and people found that the economy under state control was no guarantee against corruption.

In order to keep the floundering Cuban economy floating, Castro decided to use the ties of communism and enlist Soviet support. This brought about a hardening of opposition from the US, which had already been hit hard by Castro's nationalization drive. On 3 January 1961, outgoing president Dwight Eisenhower terminated diplomatic relations with the Cuban government. Castro retaliated by declaring in April that Cuba was now a socialist state.

The stage was now set for a showdown. The American government put in action a covert mission to overthrow the Castro regime that came to be known as the Bay of Pigs Invasion. Though Castro's government was able to put it down, he retaliated by hardening the state's communist ideology and doing away with any semblance of a democratic process in Cuba. On 7 February 1962, the US hit back with total economic embargo on Cuba. The USSR, sensing Cuba's frustration, decided to use the opportunity to bring the Cold War to its arch enemy's neighbourhood in October 1962 by positioning its missiles in Cuba, only a short distance from Florida. The US demanded its immediate removal, leading to the worst face-off of the Cold War era, known as the Cuban Missile Crisis. Eventually, a nuclear crisis was averted, with both the US president Kennedy and the USSR premier Khrushchev agreeing to back off.

Though Castro felt slighted at being kept out of the negotiations between the US and the USSR, he soon bounced back on the international stage with several initiatives to unite anti-American countries in Latin America, Asia and Africa. None were popular, and they, instead, continued to bleed the already sick Cuban economy. With the disintegration of the USSR, Cuba could no longer depend on external economic aid. Castro responded by tweaking the socialist economy to allow certain free market elements from the late 1990s. He also reached out to Cubans in the US to return to their homeland and start new businesses. The US dollar was legalized, and tourism was promoted to earn foreign exchange.

Death and Legacy

After ruling Cuba for almost half a century, Castro finally handed over the reins of the government in 2008 to his brother and nominated successor, Raul. On the evening of 25 November 2016, the ninety-year-old Cuban leader died of natural causes.

Castro's stewardship of the Cuban Revolution has earned him a place among the world's legendary leaders. When he was just thirty-two, he used classic guerrilla struggle to oust a powerful general and national leader. Under him, ordinary Cubans benefited from accessible education, universal healthcare and land reforms. On the other hand, like many revolutionaries, he turned into a dictator who crushed political opposition with brutal measures and forced thousands of Cubans to emigrate.

However, seldom has any revolutionary played as important a role in world politics in his own country as him.

Fascinating Facts

- At the El Colegio de Belén, Castro turned out to be a highly sought-after pitcher of the school's baseball team.
- According to Cuban intelligence, Castro was reportedly the target of as many as 638 assassination attempts in all. In fact, Castro once reportedly joked that if assassination attempts were an Olympic sport, he would have won a gold medal.

19. Aung San Suu Kyi

The flowers in her hair appeared to complement the beauty of the frail-looking woman with delicate features and a gentle smile. In fact, they were a perfect guise for the steely determination and adamantine strength that are characteristic of the admirable woman. Aung San Suu Kyi is at present the state counsellor, the highest executive political authority of Myanmar, formerly known as Burma. Her resolute opposition to the Myanmarese military junta finally brought about transition to an elected government in 2015. In 1991, she won the Nobel Peace Prize for her 'non-violent struggle for democracy and human rights'.

Early Life

Aung San Suu Kyi was born on 19 June 1945 in Rangoon, now known as Yangon. Her father was the legendary liberation movement leader Aung San, the chief architect of Burmese independence from British colonial rule. Before marriage, her mother Khin Kyi was a senior nurse of Rangoon General Hospital, where Aung San had been admitted to recuperate from the rigorous march into Burma. The two were married in 1942 after which she was given the honorific title of 'Daw'. Their only girl was named after both her parents—'Aung San' for father, 'Kyi' for mother, as well as for her grandma, 'Suu'.

When she was just two years old, Suu Kyi lost her father to an assassination. Thereafter, Daw Khin Kyi entered public life and officially assumed responsibility of the social planning and policy bodies. In 1960, Daw Khin Kyi was appointed Burmese Ambassador to India and young Suu Kyi moved with her mother as well. She finished her schooling in India after which she joined Lady Shri Ram College in New Delhi. Soon, though, she left for England to study philosophy, politics and economics at the University of Oxford.

In England, Suu Kyi's local guardians were Lord Gore-Booth, former British ambassador to Burma and High Commissioner in India, and it was at his home that she met Michael Aris, a scholar in the field of Tibetan and Himalayan studies. After a two-year stay in New York, during which she joined the UN secretariat as assistant secretary, Advisory Committee on Administrative and Budgetary Questions, Suu Kyi returned to England and got married to Michael on 1 January 1972.

Family Time and Studies

For the next decade and a half, Suu Kyi was busy with her studies and family. While being a mother to two sons, she continued to work, and published many historical books on Burma, Nepal, Bhutan and other Southeastern cultures. Also, around this time, she increasingly became interested in researching her father's role in the Burmese liberation struggle and the circumstances surrounding his assassination. In 1987, Suu Kyi even enrolled at the London School of Oriental and African Studies (SOAS) to work on an advanced degree.

However, her relatively idyllic life was disrupted on 31 March 1988 with a phone call from Yangon bearing the news of her mother's stroke. Suu Kyi immediately left for Burma, leaving her family behind in England.

Political Struggle

Since 1962, Burma had been a military dictatorship under General Ne Win. His resignation in July 1988 led to popular demonstrations across Yangon, demanding the return to democratic representation. By August, the uprising had spread to other parts of the country. The military, panicking at the scale of the popular, anti-junta sentiment, unleashed violence, killing thousands of protestors. Horrified at the brutal suppression, Suu Kyi wrote an open letter to the military-controlled government, asking for multi-party elections.

On 26 August 1988, Suu Kyi gave her first public speech outside Shwedagon Pagoda in which she addressed several hundred thousand people and demanded the reinstatement of a democratic government.

In response, the military came up with the State Law and Order Restoration Council (SLORC) in September. This council passed a slew of politically oppressive measures like banning political gatherings of more than four persons as well as ordering arrests and sentencing of people without trial.

With the announcement of parliamentary elections, Suu Kyi led the formation of the National League for Democracy (NLD) and began delivering speeches across the country. In her fight against the military junta, she took up the weapons of non-violence and civil disobedience. The death of her mother in January 1989 drew massive crowds for the funeral procession to whom she vowed she would continue her struggle for democracy and human rights.

The military government cranked up its violent suppression of pro-democracy supporters with thousands across the country being arrested, tortured and killed without trial. Suu Kyi's leadership of the movement was symbolically captured in the Irrawaddy Delta in April 1989 when Suu Kyi courageously walked towards rifled soldiers aiming at her.

The House Arrest Years

Realizing that it would never be able to defeat Suu Kyi in popular representation, the military government ordered her house arrest on 20 July 1989 without any charge or trial. Undaunted, she demanded to be sent to prison, where thousands of her supporters, including students, had already been incarcerated. Despite Suu Kyi's physical absence in the public space, the NLD won the May 1990 elections by a massive majority. Predictably, the military government refused to recognize the results, and continued to rule Burma, renaming it as Myanmar.

However, international recognition of Suu Kyi's courageous struggle began pouring in. In 1991, she was awarded the Nobel Peace Prize, but because of her house arrest, her husband and sons accepted it on her behalf at the 10 December ceremony in Oslo.

Pressurized by international attention on Suu Kyi's pro-democracy movement as well as US-led economic sanctions, the SLORC decided to lift her house arrest, but still forbade her foreign travel. Despite continued harassment, in 1998, she formed a representative committee that she announced was the country's legitimate parliament. Her boldness did not go unpunished—her husband was denied a visa to Burma, and anticipating that she would not be allowed to return if she left the country, neither did Suu Kyi visit him in England. Michael, suffering from prostate cancer, passed away in 1999.

In 2000, Suu Kyi was again placed under house arrest which, apart from some scattered weeks of relief, would continue till 2002. In the meantime, the military government had announced elections to be held in 2010. In order to prevent Suu Kyi fighting the elections, the junta once again brought a series of charges against her— including that of breaking the terms of her house arrest in the wake of an incident of intrusion of a US citizen in her residential complex.

The 2010 elections turned out to be a farce, as the NLD refused to participate in the backdrop of highly discriminatory laws. Nevertheless, Suu Kyi's public persona remained influential as ever, and by stages, the military-led government was forced to relax restrictions on her meeting people.

In the parliamentary by-elections of April 2012, Suu Kyi won her Yangon seat easily, and used her new-found legitimacy to push for further political reforms. Finally, the country-wide elections of November 2015 established NLD as the majority party in both legislatures. But because prevailing laws prevented anyone with a spouse of foreign origin and children holding other citizenships from becoming the head of state, her close associate Htin Kyaw was chosen as the president. Shortly afterwards, the position of State Counsellor was created by the new government and Suu Kyi was invited to assume it.

Legacy

Suu Kyi's long struggle to oust the military-led government in Myanmar is one of the most definitive examples of a non-violent revolution in modern history. Despite being faced with the might of the gun as well as discriminatory laws for over two decades, she refused to be cowed into submission, and at an even greater personal cost, was successful in steering her country towards a representative form of government.

Over the past year, however, Suu Kyi's legacy has come under a cloud owing to her ambiguous handling of the Rohingya refugee crisis in Myanmar. Independent human rights groups have accused the Myanmarese army of carrying out large-scale murders of the Muslim ethnic group, leading to their displacement to western neighbour Bangladesh. Suu Kyi has resolutely remained quiet about the humanitarian crisis, despite a damning August 2018 UN report, describing the treatment of the Rohingya people as 'genocide'.

Fascinating Facts

- Suu Kyi has spent some fifteen years under house arrest over a two-decade-plus political career.
- She is a practising Theravada Buddhist.
- Chinlone is a traditional pastime of Myanmar—it is a combination of sport and dance, but played without an opposing team!

20. Ayatollah Khomeini

The piercing eyes under bushy eyebrows gazed steadily at the lavish spectacle ahead. The display of royal ostentation and luxury tasted like bitter gall, and he promised himself all this would end some day. The man making the vow was Ayatollah Khomeini, leader of the Iranian Revolution of 1979 that would replace the centuries-old Pahlavi monarchy with a theocratic state and the first Islamic Republic in the world.

Early Life

There is some dispute regarding the exact date of Khomeini's birth. While his own birth certificate put it as 17 May 1900, his older brother Ayatollah Pasandideh indicated it was 24 September 1902. Born in the Iranian town of Khomeyn into a family of Islamic Shia clerics as Ruhollah Mūsavi, the future leader received an orthodox religious education. In 1922, he settled into his vocation of a Shiite scholar in the city of Qom, and in 1930, took on the name of his place of birth as his surname. He quickly rose through the religious ranks—in the 1950s, he became the Ayatollah, and by the 1960s, he received the title of the Grand Ayatollah, making him the highest religious authority in Shia-majority Iran.

At the same time, Khomeini incurred a huge following among ordinary Iranians to whom the benefits of a western-educated and capitalist monarchy rarely trickled down. While the Shah and his royal family lived in luxury, the poor of the country grew increasingly discontent at the social and economic inequality. Instead of addressing the rising dissatisfaction on the ground, the royalty remained disconnected and aloof.

Revolution

Not surprisingly then, Khomeini's unwavering opposition to the monarchy and the western influence it represented found many takers in Iran. The people were especially angry when Khomeini was first imprisoned and exiled for opposing the Shah's policies. Even while living in Paris in exile, Khomeini's tape-recorded address rallied the people of Iran to rise against the Shah. By late 1978, the entire country was in the grip of civil unrest, with people, and especially students, carrying out demonstrations and strikes on 16 January 1979. The Shah fled the country and the very next month witnessed Khomeini's triumphant entry into Tehran.

A referendum in December the same year put in place a new constitution, according to which Iran was formally declared a theocratic, Islamic state. Khomeini now became the supreme religious leader for life. He had already installed a government in March 1979 that was composed of Shiite clerics. Khomeini himself acted as the last word in matters of negotiation and arbitration among regional factions. Soon, though, all political opposition was wiped out by executing all of Shah's supporters, family, friends and even people who had been mere employees in the previous government.

Hand-in-hand with such political repression went social laws that banned alcohol, western music and made the veil mandatory for women. Islamic law was installed as the sole penal code, and determined all punishments.

For the world, the most dramatic impact of Iranian Revolution was the strident policy of confrontation adopted towards both, the USSR and the US, but especially towards the latter and its allies. In November 1979, Khomeini ordered the invasion of the US embassy in Tehran, and its diplomatic personnel were kept as hostages for more than a year. In 1980, a war broke out between Iran and the then US ally, Iraq, over rights to the Shatt al-Arab waterway, which continued for eight long years. The Iran-Iraq War brought home the futility of so much destruction to the Iranians. There were faint murmurs of discontent with the government. However, the Grand Ayatollah continued his iron grip on the power centre till his death on 4 June 1989.

Legacy

The Iranian Revolution was the first mass movement in the world that brought an Islamic government to power and formalized Islamic theocracy. Despite enjoying overwhelming support, Khomeini brought in place the 'Guardianship of the Islamic Jurists' or velayat-e faqih to rule the country rather than assuming dictatorship himself. This distinction allowed him complete command of all the aspects of the country without taking on the day-to-day responsibilities of governance.

The Iranian Revolution also had far-reaching consequences on the region like the rise of the Hezbollah in Lebanon, the boost to Shia rebels in Iraq, widening of the Shia-Sunni rift, but most importantly, crystallization of anti-American forces in the Middle East—all of which continue to impact regional, and by extension, global politics till this day.

Fascinating Facts

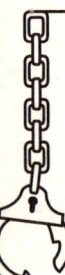

- Just five months after he was born, Ruhollah Mūsavi's father was murdered by the village landlord. The child was brought up by his mother and aunt, and then his older brother.
- During his funeral march, the shroud covering Khomeini's body was torn by the grieving masses for mementos, and his body knocked to the ground. After the crowds were controlled, Khomeini was buried in a metal coffin.

Conclusion

The Iranian Revolution has gone down in modern history as unusual in many aspects. International observers initially found it curious that a modern and secular society under the Shah willingly opted to go back to a theocratic and orthodox system. Eventually, this was linked to the rise of popular Islamic sentiment in the region, echoes of which were most recently felt in the Arab Spring phenomenon.

From late 2010, a series of anti-government uprisings engulfed states in the Middle East, starting with Tunisia, and then quickly spreading to Egypt, Syria, Yemen, Bahrain, Morocco and Libya. These uprisings were directed against the prevailing dictatorship in power, marked by protests against poor living conditions, corruption and the absence of a democracy, often spread by social media and backed by conservative Islamic forces.

Though international experts are still debating whether these uprisings can qualify for a revolution, the Arab Spring did throw up quite a few names, such as

Acknowledgements

I thank my editors Saswati and Anukta for helping me prune and polish this book to perfection.

I thank my husband for his keen insights into political movements and figures that accorded me valuable clarity.

And finally, a big thank you to my daughter for putting up with a distracted mommy during all those hours when I was at the writing table.